OPAL FROM OMAHA

OPERATION BIG ROCK BRIDES BOOK TWO

NORA NOLAN

Published by Blushing Books
An Imprint of
ABCD Graphics and Design, Inc.
A Virginia Corporation
977 Seminole Trail #233
Charlottesville, VA 22901

Nora Nolan
Opal from Omaha

Ebook ISBN: 978-1-64563-727-1
Print ISBN: 978-1-64563-728-8
Audio ISBN: 978-1-64563-729-5
VI

ONE

Big Rock, Wyoming Territory, 1885

The Ladies' Aid Society of Big Rock came to order at the sound of Harriet Smithers' whistle. She'd discovered it was the best way to get their attention.

"Ladies, ladies, we have a new prospective groom, Henry Tucker, and we've narrowed down the list of appropriate matches for him to two different young women. As you all know, our first couple match was a rousing success—" Her sentence was cut off by whoops and applause from the group. She smiled but held up her hands to get them to quiet down. "—a rousing success for Angus Kelly and his wife Nessa. His partner, Henry, wants us to find a wife for him. I guess he doesn't want Angus to be the only lucky man at the sawmill."

"You mean the only man at the sawmill getting lucky," said Bethie Hickam.

Harriet allowed them all to giggle and snicker at that. "We've narrowed down the selections to Opal McAllister, a friend of Amy Larkin's, from Omaha, and Lacy Holt, a woman from Lincoln, Nebraska who is a friend of Molly McBride. Henry is a fairly quiet man and prefers a woman who isn't given to childish silliness. He appreciates intelligence, a sense of humor, and honesty as the qualities he most desires in a spouse." Harriet smiled wryly at the group. "He made the comment that he'd never have agreed to a mail order bride if it hadn't been for seeing what we did for his friend Angus. You have it there, ladies, success begets success. Let's have another success!"

That stirred up another round of applause and yells that in any other setting would have seemed inappropriate for ladies.

"You've all read the information about these two prospective brides. I'm going to present them both to Henry, but I'm going to suggest that he write to Opal first. Does everyone agree with that? She seems right for him somehow. I'm just afraid Lacy, being a bit younger, might not yet have the maturity Henry is interested in."

All in the group nodded their agreement. "I'm sure we have a younger single man in town who might be interested in Lacy," Bethie said.

"We do indeed," Harriet said as she smiled. "I'm meeting with him after I speak with Henry. Now for the next order of business. Mrs. Worthy has taken sick and we need to organize and plan for food to be taken to them for the next few days. She's got those four sweet children and you know her husband's useless in the kitchen."

HENRY TUCKER HEADED for Mary's Restaurant to meet with Harriet Smithers. He had lingering doubts about the whole mail order bride plan, but he'd given his word and would never back out of at least giving it a try. He knew he wasn't obligated to marry; he could always provide fare for her to return home if it didn't work out when they met in person. Or they might be able to find a suitable match for the young woman from among other bachelors in town. That thought, that fail-safe, stayed in the back of his mind and comforted him.

"Hello, Henry," Harriet said as he sat down at her table. She had already ordered coffees for them both.

"Good evenin', Miz Smithers."

"Call me Harriet; everyone else does."

He smiled. "All right then, Harriet."

"I have two possible candidates who I believe match your wish list. And I'm very confident about one of them. She's a young lady from Omaha, a friend of Amy Larkin; you know, the sheriff's wife."

"How young is she?" Henry didn't want what he considered a child bride.

"I believe she's almost thirty. Is that too old for you?"

He laughed. "I'm on the middlin' to high end of the thirties myself, Miz Harriet. Her age is fine. I'd just rather not have a wife I could have theoretically fathered. At the risk of sounding too selective, most women I've met don't get interesting until they've lived a while."

She gave a low laugh. "Well, that's refreshing. Many men want them young."

"Thirty is still young. Hell, I'm still young." He grinned. "So, tell me about this lady you like for me."

"Her name is Opal McAllister. She currently works as a secretary to an attorney, has for nearly ten years now. Her parents are deceased; she lives with her brother and his wife. She's never been married but was engaged once. Her fiancé was taken by yellow fever six years ago."

"I'm sorry to hear that. It must have been painful for her."

Harriet looked up at him. "Yes, I'm sure it was. But there comes a time when mourning has to be set aside so we can move on and enjoy life. I believe that's where Opal is now, and where she's been for a time. Here's what we have in mind for Miss Opal. Amy would like to see her old friend, so she and the sheriff would like for Miss Opal to stay with them in their home until such a time as she gets married."

She flashed Henry a big grin. "Of course, that's where you come in. Amy wanted her to come right away and simply live as their guest until she found a husband, but Miss Opal wasn't comfortable with that. She said she'd feel as though she were being marketed to the highest bidder. So, we'd like for you to go ahead and write to her, exchange a few letters, and see what you think of each other. I think you'll know very quickly if she's someone you might be interested in. You might also consider going to visit with Amy and finding out all you can about Miss Opal before you write that first letter. It could give you a better foundation for your comments."

"I like that idea. I'll head over to the sheriff's office when I leave here and see about dropping in to visit Amy this evening."

"Wonderful!" Harriet handed Henry a printed list of things to discuss in his introductory letter. "This will help, too. These are things a woman wants to know. So talk about these things and add as many other comments as you'd like about yourself, and be sure to ask her questions. You want her response to have as much information and insight into her character and personality as does your letter. Have fun with composing it."

Henry took the list. "I'll do that, Miz Harriet."

He said his good bye and headed for the sheriff's office.

"AMY, I can't tell you how much I appreciate a good home-cooked meal. I guess technically mine are home-cooked, but they aren't nearly as good as yours," Henry said as he wiped his mouth.

"Then you'll be pleased to know that Opal is a good cook, too. Her pies win prizes. And she and her mother taught me how to make fudge, so that should tell you something."

"I understand her parents are gone now."

"Yes, several years ago. A buggy accident took them both. It affected Opal and her brother deeply at the time. But that was a long time ago. Wounds heal."

"I was hoping you could tell me things about Miss Opal, things about her personality and her character. I'd like to get to know her in a sense before I write to her. It may help me—I'm not big on writing about myself."

"Why the hell not?" the sheriff asked. "You sure aren't shy." He chuckled as he poured Henry some whiskey.

Henry laughed. "No, not shy, but I don't usually talk about myself so much." He shifted in his chair and leaned his hulking body over, placing his elbows on his knees as he turned his attention to focus solely on Amy. "What kind of man was her fiancé?"

Amy blew out a deep breath, remembering. "He was nice as I recall. Attractive looking, brown hair, average height, pleasant smile. Seems like his family had a small dairy farm. I remember he made deliveries sometimes when his younger brother wasn't able to. I think that's how they met. He struck me as a quiet fellow by nature, but friendly enough."

"What about Opal's personality?"

Amy smiled. "Opal was always the good girl. There were a few times I coerced her into sneaking out at night and going for walks with me. Nothing wild, but it probably wasn't the safest thing to do, in retrospect. Her mother and father would have had her hide! They were pretty protective of her. She didn't like it, but she really wasn't one to rebel much. Just our moonlight walks. She's reserved until she gets to know someone well. Then she loves to talk."

"She's a talker?" Henry asked, hiding his concern. He was definitely not attracted to silly babblers.

"We used to talk about everything. She liked philosophy. She loved reading all the philosophers. And mythology! I don't know how many hours we spent discussing Greek and Roman mythology, and some other lesser known myths from around the world. New ideas, too. She read every newspaper or periodical she could get her hands on and she liked to discuss current affairs."

"That sounds interesting to me," Henry said with a little awe in his voice. "Sounds like I'm going to have to start reading a bit more. I've gotten out of the habit since I moved out here."

Amy laughed. "You can ask her to read them to you. She has all the books. Oh, and once she knows you well, she'll unleash her sense of humor. Wicked." She shook her head. "Wicked funny."

Henry nodded his head and smiled tentatively. "A good girl who can be enticed into mischief. This woman sounds like someone I'd like to know. *Need* to know. I think I'll enjoy her company."

"I'm sure you will. She was my best friend for years. I consider that she still is, though I haven't seen her since I moved here. That's why I want her to stay with us until she's married. I can't wait to see her again."

"You know Harriet suggested that we write to each other before she comes out here. I'll post a letter tomorrow. Maybe I'll get a response in two or three weeks, if all goes well between here and Omaha, and she writes as soon as she gets my letter."

"Yes, I'm sure she will. She's probably as eager as you are. Now go home this minute and write tonight!" Amy said, laughing.

He did.

———

DEAR MISS OPAL,

Please allow me to introduce myself: I'm Henry Tucker from Big Rock. I'm thirty seven years old. My business partner found his wife through a mail order bride process and their happy success has inspired me to try to find a wonderful woman to be my wife, too.

Mrs. Harriet Smithers was excited to share your information with me; she thinks we would be a perfect match. When I talked with Amy Larkin, she described your personality and interests. Now I'm even more eager to get to know you.

I'm about six feet tall, with dark hair and brown eyes. At the moment, I'm clean-shaven, but sometimes in the fall and winter I like to grow a beard.

I was raised in a sparsely populated area west of here, in northern Nevada. My grandfather was one of the first settlers there. Years ago, he and my grandmother came in a wagon train, bound for the coast, but as they traveled through a particularly breathtaking area, several of the families decided to settle there. Life was hard for them, but they persevered and carved out a contented life. As is always the case with generations, my father's life was easier because of the efforts of my grandfather. By the time I came along, there were more settlements within traveling distance, and the railroad brought with it more civilized amenities as I grew older.

My business partner, Angus Kelly, and I own a sawmill and a furniture manufacturing concern. We make all sorts of wooden and upholstered furniture. Woodworking is something I learned from my father, and I still enjoy it. When I have spare time, I can often be found working on projects in my workshop.

I believe I'm fair-minded, and it's fair to say our employees would agree. I've made many friends here in Big Rock. I've been here for nearly three years. It's a fine little town; I think it would be a good place to raise a family. I have a home on the edge of town. If the town keeps growing as it has, it might not be the edge for very long.

My house is only meagerly furnished. I suppose I've subconsciously been waiting for a wife to put her touches on it. I have only the furniture I've found necessary. I have a table and six chairs in the kitchen, a couch, end table, and coffee table in the parlor, and a bed, nightstand, and wardrobe in the bedroom. I'm proud to say that all of it was made in our factory. I look forward to having a wife make a warm and inviting home of this place.

The kitchen is fully furnished with items that belonged to my late mother. If we pursue this union between us, you are welcome to cull any items you don't wish to keep and add items of your own, or purchase new ones. I would want it to be yours to do with as you please. I'll be happy to bow out of the food preparation arena to the extent that you wish. I have a feeling that once you witness my culinary abilities, you'll prefer it that way. Perhaps you could teach me. I'll warn you, my mother wasn't successful in doing so. Amy told me you make prizewinning pies. I look forward to those!

My businesses provide well for me, and my income is reliable. I understand you work now, but there is no financial reason that you should have to after we marry. My preference would be to have a wife to keep my home, but if you wish to continue working and there is a position in town that interests you, we can certainly discuss it. My goal is to have a happy wife.

Amy shared with me that you love discussing philosophy and mythology and subjects such as that. That enthralled me! These things interest me, too, along with religion, politics, and advances in science and medicine. I would dearly love to have a wife who enjoys such discussions.

Most Sundays, I attend our Methodist church here in town. It's the only church there is in our community. I grew up with the religious teaching of my parents; we didn't live near a church, so I never attended one until I was nearly grown. I would call their views similar to Methodist leanings. I suppose that's the benefit of being taught the Bible outside of an organized theology. As an adult, having observed other religions, I realize my parents did a sort of theological "pick and choose" when it came to my spiritual upbringing.

My parents had a wonderful marriage, and I believe, as a result, I had a mostly happy childhood. The only thing that might have improved it would have been having a sibling.

Mrs. Smithers asked me to think about what I want in a marriage and what I want my future to be like. Miss Opal, as I've gone through the exercise of writing this introduction letter, I've been forced to examine my life. I now realize how lonely it is.

I want a wife whom I love abundantly in all ways: intellectually, emotionally, spiritually, and physically. I want a relationship where we both feel loved, secure, supported, and cherished. I want a close, intimate bond with my partner in life. A man in love once told me he knew whenever his lover entered the room, whether he saw her or not. He felt her presence. Lord willing, I want a connection that close. I hesitated even sharing that with you for fear of appearing to be a hopeless romantic. I don't normally think of such things, much less speak of them.

What kind of marriage and future do you imagine when you allow yourself to daydream of the perfect one?

I eagerly await your thoughts. Please tell me every little thing about you!

.   .   .

SINCERELY YOURS,
Henry Tucker

HENRY READ the letter over and over before deciding he probably couldn't improve it much. He realized if there was something he left out, he could include it in the next letter.

TWO

Dear Mr. Tucker,

Thank you for your letter. I eagerly read it, and I've reread it several times, thinking I might learn more each time. We do indeed sound suited to each other, based on our mutual interests. I admit, I fancy the thought of discussing Nietzsche or Goethe or Old Testament prophets with you while lying on a quilt under the stars, listening to the sounds of God's creatures around us. That might sound odd and even forward, but my friend Amy used to talk me into moonlight walks, and it instilled in me a love of the nighttime sky.

I am about five feet and four inches tall, which I suppose is about average. My hair and eyes are brown, too.

I was raised in a Baptist church; my father was a deacon. We were active in church activities as you might imagine. Since the basic tenets are similar, I would have no problem attending a Methodist church.

If we choose to pursue this relationship further, I appreciate *your willingness to discuss allowing me to work. I believe that openness speaks well of your intention to make a successful union, as well as an intention to consider my feelings and wants.*

Although I enjoy my work, I don't consider that it defines me. I derive the true joy in my life from my friends and family and my interests. I, too, have thought about what I want in a marriage, and I don't think having an outside job fits well into my vision, unless it becomes necessary. My strongest desire is to be a homemaker in the truest sense, to provide a healthy, happy home for my husband and children.

As for what I want in a husband, please forgive me for being forward and even blunt. A marriage is a serious thing indeed. I'm taking leave to be explicit, for if we continue, we will live with this decision until one of us passes over. We should speak plainly of what we desire. You mentioned you might be thought of as a hopeless romantic, but I prefer to think of us as hopeful romantics.

I envision my husband as a strong yet gentle man of good humor, loving but firm with our children and with me. Some of the thoughts in my mind I don't dare mention aloud, much less commit to paper. I, too, romanticize a vision of a special connection between my husband and me. It is a love wherein we can almost read each other's mind. He has a devilish humor he shares with only me, and ideas of relations that would indeed be wicked if not for the bonds of marriage. To such a man, I will give myself freely and with great abandon.

Lest you think that by speaking of these things that I have experience in this area, I assure you I am untried. But I am not a naïve young girl; I'm a grown woman.

I've spoken of romantic love, but one of my favorite quotes is by Nietzsche: "It is not a lack of love, but a lack of friendship that makes unhappy marriages." Is it reasonable to desire that a spouse be a best friend and a passionate lover at the same time? I pray, Mr. Tucker, that it is absolutely attainable. I also pray I have not offended you by saying so.

Please, when you write back, call me Opal. Reading back on some of the scandalous comments I've made, perhaps a more inti- mate form of address is acceptable.

Do write back soon, Henry, if I may assume the more inti- mate address. After baring my soul in such a manner, I eagerly await your next letter. My worst fear is that you'll think me unac- ceptably forward and terminate our correspondence. I wait on pins and needles, with bated breath, until I know your thoughts.

Until then,
Opal McAllister

Big Rock, fourteen days later

Henry's daily inquiry at the general store about his mail finally received a positive result. His heart beat a little faster as he hurried home to read it. He poured a drink, downed it, and then poured another one before sitting down at the table and care- fully opening the envelope so as not to unnecessarily rip the paper.

As he read it, his smile grew. As he reached the last few paragraphs, he felt something else begin to grow. He read it again, particularly those last thoughts she'd shared about a phys- ical relationship. He liked what he read.

Henry thought of her fear that he would think her too forward, and he wanted to alleviate her fears as quickly as he could. He pulled out paper and a pen and ink and started to write, then realized she'd have to wait another week or two before learning he was happy with her response. He didn't want to prolong her unease.

He jumped up, went outside to saddle his horse, and took off for the telegraph office. The owner, Caleb Carter, greeted him when he came in. "How can I help you, Henry?"

"I need to send a wire to Omaha."

"Can do, my friend," he said as he handed him a form. "Fill this out and I'll get right on it."

Henry thought about what he wanted to say, all the while keeping it brief.

IN RECEIPT of letter STOP Agree with your thoughts STOP Eager to meet you STOP I'll post return letter tomorrow STOP Faithfully yours, Henry Tucker

HENRY PAID for the wire and hurried home to write the letter.

MY DEAR OPAL,

I was very happy to receive your letter. Please know that I was not in the least offended by your comments. Indeed, I was touched that you consider this process serious enough to trust me with your honest thoughts. I will hold that trust in my heart and your thoughts in deepest confidence.

I'm happy to know you would choose to spend your time as a homemaker. At the same time, I don't want you to be overburdened. My income will allow you to enjoy some things that other wives might not be fortunate enough to have. For example, there is a lovely older woman in town whose sole livelihood is taking in laundry. She is a dear woman, and I hope you don't mind allowing her to continue to do our laundry. I think you will like her.

Right now, I have a young girl, the daughter of one of my employees, who comes in once a week to do household chores such as sweeping, dusting, and straightening up. I would like to let her continue if you are amenable. Her father believes it is teaching her responsibility and I tend to agree.

Perhaps these things will allow you more time to read, enjoy friends, sew, or do whatever makes you happy.

I like the Nietzsche line you quoted. I, too, hope to marry my best friend. Which comes first, the friendship or the love? I can't say, but I look forward to discussing it with you.

Please forgive my boldness, too. There's another Nietzsche thought that comes to my mind. "The true man wants two things: danger and play. For that reason, he wants woman as the most dangerous plaything." I'm not sure exactly how he meant it, but I know the ideas I have that the comment might refer to.

It both thrills and humbles me that you are, as you say, untried. As your husband, I would strive to be worthy of that gift. I cannot say the same about my own past, and I hope you won't hold that against me. It has been quite a while since I have had the company of a woman, and should we marry, I promise to keep my vows and keep myself only to you.

But, dear Opal, understand that I have a healthy physical appetite when it comes to 'playing'. I can't say what Nietzsche meant by dangerous, but that does seem to add a titillating quality to the thought. Does that make me a 'true man' to which he referred? Perhaps. Love has different faces as we grow older; I realize that. But we are relatively young and healthy, and I fully expect sexual congress will play a great role in our relationship. I insist upon it, as I hope you will, too!

What I just wrote sounds so clinical. What I think and what I feel are much more visceral and passionate! Dear Opal, I want to hold you in my arms. I want to entwine my fingers in your soft brown hair and bring your face close so I can kiss your lips. I want to whisper in your ear the things I plan to do with your body. I want to make you moan and writhe and beg me to take you.

I have envisioned our wedding night, dear Opal. I want to make it a special memory for you, a treasure you'll hold in your heart and in your mind, just as I will.

"The best laid plans..." as they say. I had planned to wait until we'd met in person before declaring this, but, Opal, I have every intention of asking you to marry me. I would ask you outright now, but you should be able to see and meet me first before being put on the spot, so to speak. So I'll ask now that you please give it serious thought. As you mentioned in your letter, this isn't a decision to be taken lightly. I realize this isn't unexpected since the whole purpose of our communications is for possible matrimony, but I don't want you to feel pressured, and I don't want to appear to be cavalier and expect that you will automatically accept.

Opal, let me know how soon you would like to come here. I will send money for your travels. I hope it is soon. Very soon! Amy wants to see you. I know I do.

I await your response.

Earnestly yours,

Henry

HENRY POSTED the letter the next day and thought of little else for the next week or so. One evening, he dined with Angus and Nessa Kelly and spent the whole meal talking of Opal and his desire for her to marry him.

"Henry, ye ken the lass is going to marry ye," Angus said, almost laughing.

"Yes, I'm almost positive. All right, I am positive. But I wish I had more patience to wait."

"Aye, I understand." Angus winked at his wife. "Those days I spent waiting for Nessa to arrive were the longest of my life. Ye get so worked up, it's almost as though ye think time will pass faster if ye work yourself into a tizzy. It does no' work that way, Henry. Ye just have to wait."

Nessa tried to be helpful. She'd grown fond of Henry and thought of him as a good friend. "While you're waiting, perhaps you might think of something to give her to welcome her, or a wedding gift. A piece of furniture perhaps? I know your house is sparse when it comes to furniture."

"Well," Henry said, "I don't know, I already told her she can choose all the furniture."

"How about a special piece, like a quilt chest, that you make especially for her? I think any woman would appreciate that," Nessa volunteered.

"There ye go, mate, that's a fine idea," Angus agreed. "And it'll keep ye from fretting until ye hear back from her."

"All right, I think she might like that. Or a bookcase. That's it! She loves books. Amy says she has a lot of them. I'll build her a nice big bookcase."

"Henry, that sounds like a wonderful, thoughtful gift," Nessa said. "I'm sure she'll be touched that you thought of the perfect thing for her."

"Ye doona have any idea when she might arrive?"

Henry blew out a deep breath. "Angus, I have no idea. All I know is she'll be staying with Jim and Amy Larkin until we marry." He gave a rueful chuckle. "Amy's hoping for a long engagement so she can hog Opal's time and catch up. I'd like to marry the day she arrives."

Nessa grinned. "That's what we did, and it worked out well for us."

Henry gave her a mock frown. "Yes, but I only told her I *will* ask her to marry me. I didn't actually ask her straight out yet."

"Ye're a damn fool, my friend," Angus said. "Send a wire. Tell her ye'll marry her the moment she steps off the stage."

"Don't you think I should ask the question first?"

"No," Angus answered simply. "Just tell her."

Nessa smiled.

AS HE ARRIVED HOME, a rider called out his name to get his attention. It was Caleb Carter, the telegrapher.

"Henry, I have a wire for you. Hot off the machine." Caleb got down off his horse and handed the envelope to Henry. "If you want to respond tonight, I'll wait."

Henry could tell by the look on Caleb's face that the message was good news. "Come on in, then," he said, smiling and waving him inside. He opened the envelope and pulled out the paper inside.

I CAN ARRIVE in Big Rock 24th STOP Love, Opal

CALEB SAW a big grin pop out on Henry's face. Henry sat down and pulled out a piece of paper and began to write the return wire.

As he handed it to Caleb, Henry asked, "What do I owe you for the wires?"

Caleb read the response and laughed. "Nothing, man, this one's on me."

He went back to his telegraph office and tapped out the message.

WILL WIRE money tomorrow STOP Can wait no longer STOP Must have arms around you STOP We will marry 25th STOP Faithfully, Henry

THREE

Omaha, Nebraska

Opal flitted about, determining what to pack. Ben, her brother, and Zora, her sister-in-law, watched.

"Sis, I don't think I've ever seen you this nervous. Are you sure you want to agree to marry this man the day after you meet him? I still say you should stay with Amy until you know him better."

"Ben, I'm not nervous about the marriage. I'm nervous about the trip. You know I've never traveled before." She paused and looked at him confidently. "I'm very sure about the marriage."

"That does it. I'll travel with you. I don't want you alone out there on that train and then on the stage, and besides, I want to meet this man."

"Don't be silly, Ben. You can't leave Zora now. Why, the baby could come before you get back. I'll be fine. I'm nearly thirty years old, you know. Just because I'm anxious about the trip, doesn't mean I'm scared. I'll wire as soon as I arrive."

Ben sighed. "I still want to meet him."

"We'll visit, I promise. Stop worrying. Amy knows Henry,

and you know she'd never suggest a match with an unsuitable man." She laughed. "Her husband's the sheriff! She would definitely know if Henry was a bad sort. He's not. She's told me all about him."

"Well, she can't know everything about him. Men keep their secrets, you know."

She stopped packing to look at him. "That statement would include you, brother. Do you harbor dark secrets?"

"All right, point taken. My secrets are hardly dark. I'm just saying you can't know."

"By that argument, then Zora can't truly know you. Are you telling me she's in danger?"

Zora laughed and murmured something Opal felt sure wasn't meant for Ben to hear.

Opal continued. "And by that same argument, you wouldn't know his secrets even after you met him. So, my brother, you have no valid points left. You can meet him when we come to visit."

Ben gave in. "You don't need to try to pack everything to take. Just take the clothes and things you need for the next few days. I can ship everything else once you're settled in. I've got some strong crates I can use for the books. The rest of your belongings in here and some of Mother's things are all there are to be sent."

"Thank you, Ben." She walked over and kissed his cheek. "Let's make it as easy on you as we can. I'll pack my things to take with me, but we'll go ahead and pack the crates you'll ship later. Save you from having to pack them by yourself."

"All right, sis. Be sure to pack one bag with the things you'll need on the train. You can keep that one with you, and let them put the other bags in the baggage car. We'll need to pack some snacks for you, too, things that travel well. Jerky and small bread loaves, for example. The meals you get on the way might not be very satisfying. Last time I took a train, we stopped twice a day for meals. I got hungry between times."

Opal smiled indulgently at her brother.

Ben got an almost sheepish look on his face. "I'm glad the man sent money for a Pullman car fare. I admit, that speaks well of him."

"Amy tells me he's a fine man." She stepped over to Ben and took his hand. "And if he's half as fine as my brother, I'll be a lucky woman."

———

SHE PACKED two books for the trip, one of her favorites that she loved to reread and a new one. She also packed a blank journal she intended to write in, to document her experiences. She knew it would help pass time on the train, too.

Opal purchased a pretty green dress and hat to wear on the last day of her stagecoach ride, so she'd be wearing it when she first met Henry. She bought a couple of other dresses, too, but she didn't think they were quite as pretty as the green one. Ben told her that train and stage travel were both relatively uncomfortable, so she tried to select clothing that wasn't too tight or too fussy. Amy had already written to her long ago that, out west, most women didn't wear corsets, including her. At first, Opal was scandalized, then she realized how liberating that must be, and now that she was headed west, she made the determination not to even take one.

She also bought a new dress to be married in. It was nicer than the other dresses, but she felt sure she could wear it to church or to parties. That is, if they had parties in Big Rock. There was so much she didn't know about her new home. The dress was a light apricot-colored floral print, with touches of ecru inserts and a crocheted ecru lace collar, cuffs, and back button placket. The shade flattered her hair and eye coloring.

Opal had her mother's embroidered hankies, and one of those would be her something old. She knew Amy would let her borrow something. As for something new, she had the dress, but she also purchased a beautiful, fan-shaped, beige hair comb that would complement her dress. All she needed was something blue, and she figured Amy would have something that would work.

As the day neared for her train trip, she realized how much she'd miss her brother and sister-in-law. In a perfect situation, her brother would give her away at her wedding, but it couldn't be helped. Zora couldn't travel, and he couldn't leave her. Opal believed things happen as they're supposed to, even when people don't understand the reasons at the time. She didn't know the reason Ben and Zora weren't meant to be at her wedding; maybe one day she'd know.

The morning she was to leave for the train, Zora knocked softly on her door.

"Come in," Opal said, putting the last minute items in the large carpetbag she'd keep with her on the trip.

Zora entered slowly, holding her heavy belly as she'd been doing for the last couple of months. "I wanted to say a private goodbye. You know I've come to love you as my own sister."

Zora's eyes welled with unshed tears, and Opal's did too.

"What you're doing is so exciting. It's so romantic to take off on what will be the adventure of a lifetime in every sense for you. It's definitely an adventure and it will affect the rest of your life. I'm so glad you stayed with us these last few years; I trea-sure that time and the memories we've made. I'll miss you so much, my heart is hurting."

"Oh, Zora." Opal put her arms around the woman, as much as she could. "I'll miss you, too. I plan to come visit often so my little niece or nephew will grow up knowing Aunt Opal. When the child is old enough, perhaps he or she can spend summers with us."

"That would be wonderful, I'm sure." Zora pulled out a small tissue-wrapped bundle from her pocket. "I want you to have this. It was something I got when I was young, and it's one of my favorite pieces. I want you to have it. Think of me when you wear it."

Opal took the package and unwound the pretty paper. It was a small cameo brooch. "Zora, you love this pin. I can't take it."

"Yes, you can. I want you to have it. I know you'll love it as much as I do." She smiled through her tears. "Think of me when you wear it."

They hugged again. "I'll treasure this, you know."

"I know you will. That's why I want you to have it," Zora said.

Zora watched as Opal wrapped it back up, rolled it up in a stocking, and put it inside a pair of shoes in her bag, where it would be protected.

When Zora left the room, Opal sat down and thought about actually leaving and not seeing her brother and sister-in-law every day. Her life was indeed about to change drastically. She was glad she had a friend in Big Rock already and wondered about all those mail order brides who move to a new place, sight unseen, with no familiar faces. She felt very fortunate.

She smiled when it occurred to her that the cameo brooch had a blue background. *Something blue.* It made her think that Zora, and even Ben, would be with her in a sense at her wedding after all.

Ben took her to the train station and made sure her bags were placed in the baggage car. He carried her bag and, with directions from a station employee, escorted her to her unit in her car. He made sure she knew where all the amenities were, made sure she knew the porter who primarily worked her car. When the time came for him to get off the train, he fought tears.

"I hope you're happy there, sis, but if you aren't, you just have to wire me. I'll send money for you to come back home to us."

Opal was moved to tears, too. "How can I ever thank you for all you've done for me? I love you, Ben. But I know I'll be fine there, and I'll make a new home for myself. We'll write and we'll visit. Maybe when the baby's older, you could even move out there!" That made them both laugh. He gave her one more squeeze, kissed her forehead, and exited the train car. He didn't leave the platform, though, until the train had been out of sight for several minutes.

———

OPAL STARED at the passing scenery for the longest time, thoughts swimming in her head. She prayed. She thought. She questioned. Finally, she pulled out her new journal and began describing her thoughts and dreams ever since she'd first received the letter from Amy that asked her to consider moving to Big Rock to become a bride. She wrote about the letters and wires from Henry and how they made her feel. The journal was for her own memories, and she allowed herself the freedom to commit to paper even her innermost intimate thoughts. She wrote of yearning to kiss Henry, to breathe in his smell, and feel his arms around her. She explained how those thoughts affected her body. She wondered what he looked like beyond brown hair and eyes and a shaven face. Was he lean or stocky? Broad? Strong? Lanky? Muscular? Short hair or long? Thick hair or thin? Or balding? Was he handsome? She hoped he was at least pleasant looking. It seemed selfish to wish him handsome, but she wanted him to have a face she would welcome awakening to each morning.

What was his temperament like? His letter indicated he was fair-minded, so that hinted that he was probably even-tempered. She hoped he wasn't one given to quick anger, and if he did get angry, that he would be reasonable. Oh, would he ever hit her? She knew some husbands did that. She'd seen it before, even with one couple at her church. The wife was a mousy thing, and she'd seen her come to church with remnants of a black eye and bruises more than once. The woman seemed not to have much will of her own, and she often wondered what the woman could possibly have done to provoke his ire. Ben told her that the man had been 'counseled' more than once by a group of men from the church. He'd straighten up for a while. The wife wouldn't press any legal charges against him, probably out of embarrassment.

She could only pray Henry wouldn't ever react that way. She also resolved to be the kind of wife a man would be proud of so he wouldn't have any reason to be disappointed in her or angry with her.

The ladies auxiliary at her church often had get-togethers, and sometimes the informal conversations turned to the discussions of husbands. That's how she'd first learned of the woman whose husband beat her. It was also the first time she learned that some women weren't beaten, but were punished in other ways when their husbands were upset with them. One friend was prohibited from going anywhere except church services for a specified period of time as a punishment. One was made to stand in the corner for a time each evening after supper for a week. And a few were spanked. She'd hidden her surprise when she heard that, but knowing the women who admitted it, she thought she understood. They weren't the most well-behaved of women.

What would Henry do? *I'll be exemplary, and I won't have to worry about it.*

As the rivers and plains and forests passed by, Opal pondered and wrote about the whole marital dynamic. The Biblical idea that two would be one was an interesting one. She understood how they would physically cleave together and for that time, be *one*. But how do husbands and wives set aside their senses of self and become one in spiritual or emotional identity? Didn't the Bible mean that, too?

Before long, the porter walked through, explaining that there would be a dinner stop in twenty minutes. They would all disembark and eat, then re-board as quickly as possible to keep the train on time. The food stop also had suitable food they could purchase to have on the train if they wished.

There were two other sleeping units in her car. The one on the far end was used by a lovely couple named Millford, and their eighteen-year-old twin daughters, Ruth and Rebecca, were in the unit next to Opal. The family sort of adopted her the first day and always invited her to dine with them. They were going all the way to San Francisco, and Opal was grateful to have company for the duration of her trip.

When the Millfords found out Opal was a mail order bride, they were fascinated. It became the subject of many discussions. Opal let them know her situation was slightly different in that she already had a friend in the town who knew her groom, so she wasn't going to be thrown completely into a foreign situation. Still, the Millfords thought she was a brave young woman, particularly the twins. They thought the idea was exotically romantic.

"Haven't you wondered what he looks like?" Ruth asked excitedly.

"Ruthie," Mrs. Millford gently chided, smiling, "a man's character matters far more than his looks."

"I know, but if it were me, I would wonder."

Opal laughed. "Yes, I have wondered. I know he has brown hair and brown eyes and is clean shaven. My friend Amy told me that he's an attractive man. That's really all I know."

"You surely are brave," Rebecca said as she shook her head. "Just think—traveling all this way to marry a man you never met! I think I would be a nervous wreck."

Opal put her hand on Rebecca's arm. "That's why I'm grateful for you and your family on this trip. I was afraid it would be a long, lonely, dreadful trip, and you all are making it delightful. I thank you all for that."

"My dear," Mrs. Millford said, "you will make a lovely bride. I wish you didn't have another two days by stage after you depart the train. We could meet the young man that way. Once we get settled in San Francisco, if I send you a note with our address, would you write to us?"

"Oh, yes, I promise to do that!"

THE TRAIN TRIP, even with the company of the Millfords, seemed interminably long to Opal. She couldn't read her books with her usual attention, and she found herself having to reread passages several times before she gave up and stared out the window at the passing scenery. *If only the days could pass as quickly.*

Finally the day came when they'd arrive in Rawlins. It was also a lunch stop, so she shared one last meal with the Millfords before she said her goodbyes to the ladies. Mr. Millford, who had become fond of Opal, made sure her baggage was removed, showed her where to buy additional food for the stagecoach trip, reminded her to fill her canteen, and reminded her to keep her valuables close to her or hidden inside her clothes if possible.

Stage travel held more dangers than train travel. The stage bound for Big Rock left early in the afternoon, so she didn't have to spend the night in Rawlins. She was glad. One more night, and she would meet her intended. The butterflies in her tummy settled somewhat when she told herself that even in the worst case scenario, even if she chose not to marry Henry, she'd still be able to visit with a dear friend. That alone was worth the trip.

FOUR

The stage office wasn't terribly far from the train station, but transport was arranged for the transferring passengers and baggage. Opal was grateful that the stage wasn't overbooked, and she wouldn't be squeezed against other passengers. She knew that sometimes they were so crowded that some people had to ride on the top of the stage with the luggage. Ben had made sure she had a bag especially for the stage that was not so large that she might have to put it atop the coach. It held only the things she'd need for the next two days. Fortunately, she had enough time to put some items in her big trunk and get items out that she'd need. She felt as prepared for the stagecoach ride as she could be.

There would be several stops along the way for the stage to make. The coach could only go two or three hours before they needed a fresh team of horses, and a couple of those stops included meals for the passengers. They would spend one night in Cooper's Gap, where they'd be served a quick breakfast in the morning. From Cooper's Gap, there would be a quick stop at Williston for horses, then the next stop would be her new home.

When the station master made the announcement, Opal

boarded the stage with the other passengers. The stage had three seats, and only one person needed to sit on the middle bench. It didn't have a backrest, and the three men on the stage agreed to take turns sitting there. Opal wondered aloud if that was a normal practice. One of the men, clearly a seasoned stage rider, said it was not. He said on some trips he'd been on, people would rudely push themselves to the front of the boarding queue to claim one of the four bench seats by a window.

Opal reasoned aloud that if the three men were going to be nice enough to take turns on the uncomfortable bench, they should be able to occupy a window seat when they weren't at the bench. The ladies agreed and also agreed to take turns themselves at the remaining window seats. The man who had spoken about his experience said, "This is shaping up to be the most pleasant trip I've taken. I don't think I've ever seen such cooperation. Normally, passengers are strangers when they get on and still strangers when they get off." He laughed. "We've already spoken more in these few minutes than were spoken on the whole of the last trip I took."

The driver was an older man who called the seasoned traveler by name. It was clear the passenger took this route often. There was a younger man, armed with a rifle and wearing a pair of pistols, who sat next to the driver. She noticed another rifle and a shotgun on the floor at the men's feet. Opal learned that the purpose of the man who *rode shotgun* was to keep a wary eye out for danger and to protect the passengers and cargo in the event they were attacked or robbed.

When the trip was underway, the talkative man who traveled often introduced himself as John Keppler. He explained his business took him to the fort and on to the next town, Kerrsville, several times a year.

Each passenger in turn gave his or her name, and conversation naturally ensued.

Mr. and Mrs. Dean and their young teenage daughter were headed to the next town after Big Rock, so they had one additional day to face aboard the stage. Opal didn't envy them that.

One couple, Mr. and Mrs. Tatum, were visiting Big Rock to see Mrs. Tatum's older brother, Clint Keller, who, with his wife Shirley, owned the general store.

When it was her turn, Opal shared her name and explained, "I'm a mail order bride from Omaha. The day after I arrive in Big Rock, I'm to marry a man named Henry. I've never met him, but I have a friend in the town who knows him."

That stirred up a good bit of conversation, particularly among the women. There were a few periods of quiet among the passengers, but more often than not, there was conversation.

They learned that young Meredith Dean was an accomplished pianist and was going to be in a prestigious competition in a few weeks. They were headed to Kerrsville on this trip to check up on a job prospect for Mr. Dean.

The Tatums had returned a few months ago from a trip to several countries in the Orient, and they shared several tales of exotic foods, strange cultural customs, and peculiar animals. Mr. Tatum had the group in hysterics when he regaled the story of how one man in India wanted to purchase his wife. "As sorely tempted as I was after she spent all that money in Bangkok, I decided to keep her."

Opal hoped the Tatums stayed in Big Rock long enough to visit with them more. She found she enjoyed their company.

When they arrived at Cooper's Gap, they were a tired lot. The stage ride had been far more uncomfortable and dustier than Opal had imagined. Before supper, the ladies managed only to wash their faces and hands. When they expressed a desire to wash more, the station master's wife said they could borrow her tub, but they would have to share water. The women good-naturedly agreed.

Opal seemed the cleanest, so she went first; she hadn't sat by a window the entire day and was a bit less dusty. She washed quickly, wanting to leave the water still hot enough for the other women. After she dried off, she put on a nightgown and wrap and was shown to the area where the women would sleep.

Before she retired, she went through her things and prepared for morning. She set out the dress she'd wear and a clean shift, petticoat, bloomers, and stockings. She felt the cameo wrapped inside one of the stockings and impulsively pinned it to the shift she'd wear the next day so it would stay close to her heart. She would have worn it on her dress, but she thought the colors clashed.

Having heard some of the tales the men told earlier of robberies, she took about half of the paper money she had left and pinned it to her petticoat. Her logic was that if they were robbed, the robbers wouldn't believe she traveled with nothing, so she left some money in her reticule. She'd hate to be robbed of everything. She'd hate to be robbed, period, but if it happened, she was determined to treat it as just part of her big adventure. Then she quickly prayed for continued safe travels.

Opal pulled out her journal and sat on her cot. She wrote until all the women were bathed and joined her in their alcove, and still she wrote more. She wanted to remember these people and this trip forever. Sleep found her with her journal still in her hand.

THE NEXT MORNING WAS HECTIC. They were awakened by the smell of coffee while it was still dark. The ladies all dressed together, helping each other as they did. Opal took extra care with her new green dress, and the ladies, excited that Opal would meet her fiancé today, made sure her hair looked particularly nice with her new hat. Mrs. Tatum made the wry but funny comment that they would all dust her off at the very last minute before the stage stopped in Big Rock.

The stationmaster's wife prepared a hearty breakfast of biscuits, bacon, sausage, fried potatoes, and scrambled eggs, and it was obvious she had it down to a science. Everything came to the table hot and delicious.

On the stage, it was Opal's turn to sit by the window. Next to her was Mrs. Tatum, then Mr. Tatum sat by the other window. It was Keppler's turn on the bench in the middle. The Dean family occupied the other seat, with Meredith and Mr. Dean sitting at the windows. The stationmaster's wife sent left-over biscuits and bacon with them in case anyone wanted a snack before they made it to Big Rock. The biscuits sat in a tow sack in the middle seat beside Mr. Keppler.

Before the stage moved, Opal took out her journal and made a quick entry. "Today's the day! Perhaps the most important of my life." Then she tucked it back in the bag at her feet.

As they pulled away from Cooper's Gap, Opal's mind was on one thing: meeting Henry. She would be happy to see Amy, too, but that held no surprises for her. Henry was foremost on her mind.

What would be the first thing he'd say to her? What should she say to him? Would he kiss her today, or wait until tomorrow? He said he was eager to hold her in his arms. Would he embrace her, perhaps passionately, when they first met, or would he observe proper social decorum? She tried to think of proper yet personal things she might say to him. *I'm so happy to finally meet you in person. It's so good to finally see you. I'm so happy with how things have worked out for us. It pleases me that you want to marry quickly. I've dreamed of being a bride since I was a young girl—thank you for making that wish come true. My deepest desire is to be the wife you've always wished for.*

She couldn't decide what she'd say. Opal held no illusions that she was any true beauty. She'd always felt a bit on the boring brown side. As a teenager, she'd wanted red hair and blue eyes, or coal-black hair and green eyes, or something, anything that made her special. But no, she was just average Opal. There wasn't much to distinguish her from all the other girls. She was average in height, average in build, average in looks, shy until she knew someone well, and she was afraid even her excessive love of reading made her boring. She knew it was her own fault; through the years, there had been many times when she'd been invited to an outing but had turned it down because she wanted to finish a good book. Looking back now, she wished she had accepted those invitations.

Even so, she'd made friends. Amy was one. She'd met most of them through her church, and the rest of them she'd met from her job as an attorney's assistant.

"Opal! Opal, dear, you must be dreaming about your fiancé," Mrs. Tatum said, chuckling.

Opal laughed a little. "Yes, I was."

"Are you having second thoughts?" Mrs. Dean asked.

Opal smiled at them. "No, no second thoughts. Just eager to finally meet him, I suppose."

Mr. Dean jumped in. "Miss Opal, I promise you that man feels just the way you do. I imagine right now, he's tied up in knots, eager to meet his bride. I'm sure he's thinking of nothing else. And I can tell you this, when he sees how lovely you are, he's going to count himself very lucky."

She smiled gratefully but knew in her heart he was being kind.

FIVE

They rode in silence for a while until Mr. Keppler broke it.

"I've ridden this stage a few times. The next way station is at Williston. There's really nothing to the place. I don't think you could even call it a settlement, just the lean-to where they keep the fresh horses. When these horses are rested, they'll be ready for the next stage. I think there may be a cabin or two dotted around. One's used by the man hired by the stage company to tend the horses. Last couple of times I came through, it was a fellow named Birdwhistle. I thought that was such a lyrical name, and memorable. Older fellow, thick gray hair, and quite pleasant. I hope he's still here."

A discussion of interesting names ensued, and some of them had the group chuckling.

Suddenly, there were three strong knocks on the coach wall behind the Tatums, by the man riding shotgun, and a shout of, "Grab a gun if you got one!"

Mr. Keppler reached inside his vest and produced a pistol. "Damn!"

"What's happening?" a couple of the women asked in a panic.

Keppler answered, "The stage is carrying a special shipment of money to Kerrsville on this run. Word must have got out."

The people were jostled inside the coach when the driver stopped as abruptly as the horses could halt. The Tatums huddled together, as did Mrs. Dean and Meredith. Mr. Dean quietly reached into his valise and pulled out a revolver. He kept it concealed between his thigh and the wall of the coach.

From outside, they heard a gravelly English accent. "Throw down that strongbox! Jed, you and Red Eye, get their wallets and jewelry."

The door of the coach opened, and two men peered in. The one who stood squarely in the door held a rifle, and the other stood to the side and held two handguns. The one with the rifle stepped up on the first step and held out his hand for the valuables.

"We'll take that iron, too, mister," one of the men said to Keppler, nodding toward his pistol, "right along with your wallet."

Meredith Dean openly cried and huddled in her mother's embrace. Her mother tried to calm her by rubbing her back and quietly *shushing* in her ear, the same way she probably did when Meredith was a baby.

Mr. Tatum handed over his wallet with no argument. His wife handed over her necklace and wedding rings. Mr. Dean held out his wallet, too, not wanting to draw attention to the gun at his side.

They heard more shouting and gunfire from outside. Opal heard a groan, then the sound of a body hitting the ground. She figured the man riding shotgun had fallen since it sounded like the body fell to that side. There were more gunshots, and she knew the driver was shooting back.

One of the shots must have hit the driver, because the next thing she felt was a sway of the coach as someone stepped up onto the driver's step. She heard him open the box under the driver's seat and say something as he handed it down to another man. She heard the gravelly voice with the English accent. "Here, take this, Herman. Fasten it on to my horse."

She heard the other man mumble something, but she sensed that he'd taken the box and turned away.

Inside, all the women were now in even more of a panic. Mr. Tatum tried to calm them, telling them to give over their valuables; nothing was more important than their lives. The man who had the two handguns stepped up and pointed one of them and agreed. "That's right, give it to us, ladies. Let's make this as easy as we can."

Opal handed over her reticule but kept her eye on the pistol waving at them. Mrs. Tatum and Mrs. Dean did the same. Meredith didn't carry one and had no valuables to turn over. Opal was glad she had pinned some of her money to her clothing.

A voice called from outside, "We got it; let's get the hell outta here!"

Mr. Keppler fired a shot at the man with the rifle, who still held the women's handbags. He hit him in the face and the man fell directly down and back off the stage step.

Keppler turned his gun to the other man, but the other man was quicker. The man with the handguns shot, hitting him twice. Keppler twisted slightly and fell directly on top of Opal, who sat in the farthest corner. His head landed on her shoulder, partly obscuring her face, and his body covered most of her right side. All the women screamed, including Opal, who cringed and tried her best to scrunch herself up and shrink into the corner. They knew Keppler was dead.

"Malachi, they kilt Red Eye!" yelled the man with pistols.

While the other robber stepped over the rifleman's body to get to the door, Mr. Dean stood, positioning himself to shoot.

"Kill them all, Jed!" came the response from Malachi.

The robber jumped to the top step and fired before Dean could pull the trigger. He'd been standing at the far end of the bench seat, so he also fell onto Opal. One arm landed around Keppler. The women screamed louder. He shot Dean again. This time, Jed saw Opal's body go limp under the fallen man. "How about that?" he said. "Two bodies on one bullet."

The man in the doorway flashed a sinister grin to the women. "Sorry, ladies. You heard the man."

He quickly shot Meredith and Mrs. Dean in the head, then he shot each of the Tatums in the heart. He blew the smoke from the pistols, proud of himself for the increase in his body count. Walking to the front of the stagecoach, he said, "All dead, Malachi. I got their valuables in this sack."

Malachi Stone took the bag and said to the other man in his gravelly accent, "Herman, go make sure."

"Yes, sir, boss."

Herman stepped around to the side where the door was and stuck his head inside.

He shot all around with his revolver. He was unable to get a clear shot at Opal's head or heart, but he had a clear shot at her arm and decided to shoot her shoulder. She didn't flinch.

"They're all gone, boss."

"Good. Let's get the hell out."

———

OPAL CAME TO, aware of pain and a weight on her. She couldn't move and had difficulty breathing and at first couldn't figure out why. Disoriented panic threatened to overcome her, but she forced herself to take even, shallow breaths. She was alive.

She couldn't remember everything, but she did remember

the two men with guns, especially the one who shot Keppler. She got a good look at him. She had no idea how long they'd been gone, or even how long she'd been unconscious. She felt queasy at the smell of so much blood and death and tried to reach for her canteen. Of the two men who'd fallen on her, Dean's body was in her way, blocking her from the canteen. After a few minutes, she knew she had to act. She couldn't wait any longer—she was afraid she'd pass out again.

When she tried to lift her left arm, she felt an intense pain centered in her shoulder. Opal was able to move her right arm, but the movement made her aware of aggravated pains on her right side just above her waist.

She knew she had to move the men whose bodies weighed her down. With her right arm, she pushed at Dean. His body shifted for a moment but fell back into the same place. She'd have to push harder. She tried to take a deep breath, but it was hard with their weight on her and with the pain in her side. Opal steeled herself and pushed with her right hand, grunting in pain as she did. Dean slipped down about three inches and a couple of inches over. But still, he was on her.

Opal had to take a few moments to catch her breath and get past the acute pains she felt at that movement. When she was ready, she heaved and pushed at him again. This time, he fell but was caught on his knees, still mostly upright against the wall of the coach. She pushed him over and steeling herself again, moved her feet out from under him.

She was able to breathe a little more deeply, but it intensi-fied the pain in her side. If she had to make a choice between breathing and pain, she'd have to endure the pain.

The strap on the canteen had been tucked under her legs, and she found it. She was able to pull it up and out from under Dean's side. Opal took small sips, only wanting enough to slake the awful thirst and parched mouth. She felt like she must have swallowed all the dust in the coach. She didn't want to make herself more nauseated, so she took only a few tiny sips.

She sat still for a few minutes, taking stock of her situation. She was the only one left alive. The sight of the bodies around her was horrifying, but she knew she couldn't think of that right now if she were going to survive. She *would* survive. She had to get herself up on the driver's seat and take this stage on to Williston, then to Big Rock. Maybe Mr. Birdwhistle at the next stop would help her drive on into Big Rock after he changed the team. If he was as nice as Keppler said, she felt sure he'd take over and let her rest until they got to town. And to Henry. And to medical care.

Opal looked then at what was left of Keppler's face and knew what she had to do. She lifted up her right hand and pushed at his midsection. He moved, but not enough to free up her torso and left leg. She would have to push his shoulder—the one where so much blood and tissue from his face had fallen. She closed her eyes and pushed as hard as she could since he was on her left and she could only push with her right hand. It hurt her side to exert.

That effort pushed him over mostly onto Mrs. Tatum. Opal watched in detached revulsion as the momentum he got from her push made him inch down Mrs. Tatum's body, finally crumpling to the floor.

She sat still to breathe and steady herself again. With her good right hand, she looped the strap of her canteen around her neck and over her shoulder. The distance between her and the door looked deceptively short, and she knew it. She was weakened, and there were dead bodies in her way. If she could sit on the middle bench and swing her legs to the other side, she'd have an easier path to step since there were no bodies in the floor on that side.

Opal took the deepest breath she could and, taking hold of

the window frame, pulled herself up. The sudden change made her dizzy and she fell back to her seat. The exertion made her shaky, and the sudden movement and jerk of the drop back onto the seat sent a jolt of pain from her wounds. She sat again for a few moments and changed tactics. She wouldn't try to stand. Looking at the middle bench, she stood only enough to shift her bottom around nearly one hundred eighty degrees and dropped onto the seat. From there, she 'walked' her legs around to the other side, where she scooted herself inch by inch along the bench until she reached the end of it near the door. She did her best to avoid touching the legs and feet of Meredith and Mrs. Dean.

She remembered and, looking down now, confirmed that there were only two steps before hitting ground, and the bottom step was a long way from the ground. The bench she sat upon stopped a few inches into the coach, so that part of the floor was essentially another step at the top. The first step down *outside* the door was wide enough for both feet to stand, but it wasn't terribly deep. The next step was a very small one, only large enough for part of one foot.

Afraid she'd pass out if she tried to stand again, Opal poised her feet above the wide outside step, in hopes that they'd land there, and held on to the side of the doorway. She half-lowered and half-dropped to her bottom on the floor as gently as she could, but the impact jarred her so that the pain took her breath away again. It hurt so much that her eyes watered.

She was sweating as much from her body's reaction to her injuries as from her exertion. She knew she was in trouble and took another sip of water to fortify herself. She wiped the sweat from her brow.

Opal sat on the floor of the coach and planned her next move. She would lower her bottom to the wide step. It was a shorter distance and shouldn't be as hard on her as dropping from the bench to the coach floor. *I can do this.* Her right foot was over the tiny bottom step; she could almost reach it. She held her left leg loosely, prepared to put her weight on it to catch herself if something went wrong and she didn't land squarely on the wide step.

Opal grabbed the door frame again, lower this time, trying to hold as much of her weight with that arm as she could. With a little groan, she propelled her bottom and held onto the doorway for dear life. She made it to the wide step, breathing heavily. Sweat dropped into her eyes and she wiped them with her sleeve. Now both of her legs dangled and didn't touch the ground—or the dead body on the ground.

She'd have to plan her next move carefully because of the distance to the ground and the dead man. The ground was several inches from her feet, and she studied the places where she could see ground below rather than dead body. If she could hold her weight on the door frame again enough to lower herself as she twisted to the right, she could be clear of the body.

Opal said another quick prayer, grabbed the door frame with her right hand, and pushed off. The pain made her shout, but the next thing she knew, she was upright, her feet were on the ground, and she was leaned over the wide step, her upper body's weight mostly supported and steadied by her right arm that rested on it. Her heart beat wildly.

She stood there, eyes closed, until she managed to calm herself again. In a few moments, she again felt sweat dripping down her face, and she lifted her head and wiped with her right sleeve before opening her eyes.

Now she had to figure out how to get up on the driver's seat, but she couldn't from this vantage point because the open coach door obscured her view. She'd have to get it closed, and to do that, she'd have to move out of the way.

Opal reached under the open door as far as she could, to get better leverage, and pulled the heavy thing toward her. When her body was the only thing keeping the door from closing, she inched her way backward, leaning her body as much on the wagon wheel as she could with that shoulder injured. When she cleared the doorway, she pulled the door into position until it clicked into place.

Earlier, she had fleetingly wondered why the horses hadn't been frightened at the gunfire and run off, pulling the coach along dangerously. Now with the door closed, she saw to her dismay the reason why. The body of the man riding shotgun was doubled over on the ground, wedged under the right front wheel. It looked as though the horses might have tried to run but couldn't because she didn't think a man who just fell could be wedged like that. Her chin drooped and shoulders slumped when she realized she'd have to summon the strength to pull him out.

Leaning against the stagecoach and trying to reach across her body with her right arm for support, she took tiny steps. She tried her best to step around the dead man when she could, but she had to take a couple of steps on his body. When she was leaning on the front part of the front wheel, she stopped to assess her situation again.

The horses hadn't been able to pull the stage over the doubled-up body. She was afraid that as soon as she moved it, they might still spook. She'd need to set the brake as soon as she moved the body in case they did. He was wedged in there well, so well that his clothing and perhaps a bit of his body were under the wheel. The horses would have to back up before she'd be able to clear him. She didn't think she had the strength to stand next to the horses, soothe them, and pull them backwards. The reins had fallen to the ground behind the horses. *Oh Lord, how am I going to get those reins?*

She couldn't bend over, and there was no way she could

reach them. Opal picked up a rifle that had been under the driver's feet; it was the only thing long enough to reach the reins from where she stood. She held it near the butt and stretched out her arm, leaning in. It was heavy and she concentrated on not dropping it, no matter how it hurt her side. She was able to drag the reins toward her, gathered in one place. Then she got the heavy rifle under them and began lifting as fast as her side pain allowed her to and got them resting over the bar in front of the driver's box. She stood there a minute, leaning on the wheel, then put the rifle back on the floorboards. Holding the heavy long gun like that had sapped her strength. It would have been awkward even if she hadn't been shot.

She needed to back up the horses about four or five inches. Once that was done, she'd immediately have to set the brake. If the horses got spooked and ran, it would likely mean death for her, being left behind. There was no way she could chase after them.

Opal was still leaning against the wheel. She knew she couldn't do that while it backed up, so she straightened up, standing on her own power for the first time since she'd exited the coach. She stood still for a bit to make sure she wouldn't get dizzy or pass out.

She grasped the reins and gently took up the slack. The horses must have sensed something because they started getting restless.

"Come on, horses, you get to save the day now," she said softly. The horse nearest her turned his head to her briefly, then reared his head up and then back and forth. That seemed to stir the other three and they started to appear agitated.

"That's it, I know you can hear me. Let's all calm down. We just need to stick together now. I really need for you all to be on my side here and work with me, so we'll all be safe," she continued, cooing. She began to sing the first song that came to her mind, *Come, Thou Fount of Every Blessing.* Although it was causing her pain to sing, the sound seemed to settle the horses and the words comforted her. She kept singing.

She held the reins steady in her right hand, her left one dangling at her side because of the pain in her shoulder. She kept singing and pulled back gently on the reins. The horses stepped about fitfully but managed to step backwards a few inches in the process, just enough. Opal gave a mighty groan on some of the words she sang as she pushed the heavy brake bar against the wheel. Because she was standing to the side as she held the reins, the coach had angled ever so slightly, but that was no problem. She stopped again to regain what little strength she had, still singing in a very faint voice.

The body under the wheel moved more easily than she expected; she was able to knock him over, and it took surprisingly little effort to roll him over a few more inches with her foot until he was just out of the path of the wheels. Now she only had to climb up onto the seat. *It looks so high from here!*

She decided she would try to use the wheel spokes as rungs on a ladder. She could climb up, and if she gauged the height correctly, when she stepped up high enough, she could lean over the low driver seat rail to keep from falling in case of a misstep. That is, provided it didn't press into her wounded side.

She tossed her canteen up on the floorboards, then with her right hand, she grasped a solid handhold above and lifted her foot. Her skirt got in the way. She thought a few moments, then pulled up the front of her skirt and petticoats and tucked them in her waistband.

The front and back wheels on this coach were the same size, large. With her hand solidly holding on, she stepped up on a spoke that was about ten inches off the ground with her right foot and pulled herself up. She let her left foot find a corresponding spoke on the other side of the hub and took the deepest breath she could manage. Just holding on aggravated the pain in her side, but she had no choice.

Opal had to take it slowly; using her right hand for support as much as she had to had caused great pain to the wounds on her side. She moved her right foot up one spoke and then let the left foot do the same. Encouraged by that small success, she went ahead and moved her right foot up two spokes, realizing she needed to be extra careful since it was at a diagonal angle. It wouldn't do for her foot to slip down to the hub and jar her; she might fall. Her left foot found the corresponding spoke on the other side and she stopped to breathe again. The pressure she had to place on her legs made them even more shaky and unsteady.

She needed to find a higher handhold. Opal reached as far as she could and grasped the wagon seat as quickly as she could so she wouldn't fall backward. She'd have to ignore the driver's hand that lay lifeless near hers.

Opal thought if she put her left foot up on top of the wheel, she should be able to make a big step up and hoist her top half over the rail. One problem was that the driver had fallen to his side and he still lay in her way with his head at the same rail. She'd just have to get over and around him.

She took several small calming breaths and prayed she wouldn't fall. *Sweet Jesus, please get me up in that seat. Give me your mighty strength and guide my hands and feet.*

She hadn't expected the intense pain she felt in her side. She screamed through it and hurled herself over the rail. It hit her lower on her belly than the gunshot wound, so that was one small blessing.

Her weight was entirely on the bench, so she no longer felt any fear of falling. But she was lying across the body of the dead driver. Still holding on to the bench with her right hand, she had to contort herself to place her right foot on the floorboards to her right. Once it was there, she closed her eyes and pushed against it. She scooted herself several inches.

While she could still reach it with her right hand, she leaned across the driver's body and disengaged the wheel brake.

One more mighty push with her foot and she was clear of the driver, with both knees on the floorboards, her chest on the bench.

She sat there a few moments before attempting to lift into a sitting position. She saw the reins and was grateful they hadn't fallen again; maybe her guardian angel had held them there. She took them and tucked them under the driver's body so they wouldn't become dislodged with her efforts.

She pushed off the bench with her hand and rose. She turned and sat, took as deep a breath as she could, and then pulled the reins into her hands.

Thank you, Lord, now please get me to Williston before I pass out.

Opal put her hand to her side and realized how badly she was bleeding. A glance to her right showed her the trail of blood she'd left. She untucked the skirts from her waist and using her left arm as a weight holding the fabric, ripped the wide bottom ruffle off both the petticoats. Getting all the way around them was painful and tedious. They were full enough, and she managed, with difficulty, to get them wrapped around her several times and tucked in securely. The pressure felt good against her sides as though it helped prop her up.

Opal had to rest a few minutes after that exertion. When she was ready, she gave the horses a *hyah* and gently whipped the reins. They began to walk, and Opal finally let herself feel some hope. She urged them into a trot, and went at that pace until she knew how her pain would be affected. She let them gallop on the long straightaways, only slowing them when she saw a rut in the road. She learned the hard way how much that hurt. Stagecoaches weren't built for smooth rides even in the best of circumstances.

Only two more stops. One stop for horses, and then it's straight home after that. My new home.

Opal forced herself to think about Henry waiting for her at the stagecoach station, eager to hold her in his arms. Maybe he'd kiss her. Maybe he'd hug her. The thought hit her that she must look awful after all this. What would Henry think? She looked down.

Damn. She was bleeding through the bandages. There would be no romantic meeting for her and her fiancé. Would he still want her? Her body would bear scars now. Surely, he'd still want her. No man would let that keep him from marrying. Would he? No, not her Henry. She felt sure he wasn't that fickle.

It wasn't too long before she saw the roof of a lean-to and knew she'd reached Williston. *I made it!* A low chuckle escaped her, and she knew it was a nervous release of her built-up fear and tension. It grew to as big a laugh as the pain in her side allowed. She called out *whoa* to the horses as she pulled on the reins to make them stop.

"Mr. Birdwhistle," she called out as loudly as she could. "I need your help." She looked around, having expected him to come running up more quickly than this. The other way station men had all been standing at the ready with fresh horses as soon as they heard the approaching coach.

Opal looked across the yard, straining to focus her bleary eyes. There, on the ground near the lean-to, lay a dead man, an older man as Keppler had described. His head was turned to the side and she saw his eyes were open in a frozen grimace. There were two red stains on the back of his shirt.

"Oh, no, Mr. Birdwhistle."

For the first time since she'd come to in the stage with the weight of two dead men on top of her, Opal cried. She couldn't help it. She cried for the driver and the man riding shotgun, she cried for young Meredith, she cried for the other new friends she'd made on the trip, she cried for Birdwhistle, and she cried for herself. She sobbed for quite a while.

Finally, she stopped. She wiped her nose and tears with one of her petticoat tails, what was left of it. Opal found her canteen and took a few more small sips.

Think, girl. You can do this. You're only two, maybe three hours away from Henry. You can endure anything for three hours.

She didn't have the energy or strength to change the horse team, even if she knew how, which she didn't. This team would just have to take them on into Big Rock. There was no other choice. She'd have to take it more slowly, though, so as not to hurt the beasts more than they could stand.

They started out at a walk for a long time. Opal hoped that would rest them a bit, and they seemed to be doing all right. She gave the reins a little shaky whip and they quickened their pace. She kept them at this pace for a while then slowed them again when she realized she was getting dizzy. She looked down and saw the blood still oozing out of her wound despite the bandage she'd applied. Her shoulder wound was bleeding, too. She'd thought it had stopped for a while.

Please Lord, let me get to Big Rock. I need your help. Keep me conscious. Send me your angels, Lord! I ask you to deliver me from this. Please deliver me to Henry. Alive.

She repeated the prayer continually as she rode, in different words, in the same words, silently and aloud.

HENRY HAD WAITED PATIENTLY for the first thirty minutes the stage was late. The stationmaster assured him it was probably just something simple like a broken wheel and they'd be along soon.

Now, over an hour had passed. Henry, the stationmaster, Sheriff Larkin and his wife Amy, Clint Keller, and Deputy Aaron Glover all waited anxiously, steadily growing more worried.

"I'm not waiting anymore," Henry said. "I'm going out to meet 'em."

"I'll ride with you," Sheriff Jim said. "Amy, you can wait here," he added as he set foot in the stirrup and pulled himself into his saddle.

"I'll do no such thing, and you can't stop me, so don't even try."

Under the circumstances, Jim understood her worry. He didn't object when she hopped up on the wagon they had waiting that was supposed to carry Opal and her bags, and *hyahed* the horses into action.

"Oh hell," the deputy said, "that stage has never been this late before. I'll go, too. You all get started; I've got to go out back and saddle my horse. I'll catch up." He lived in the house directly behind the jail and the stage office, so he didn't have to go far. If he cut through his own back yard and the forest and field behind it, he'd be able to catch up with them.

Henry led the way, with Jim a couple of hundred feet behind him. He lagged back to be nearer to Amy in the slower-moving wagon. The deputy passed Amy and Jim and was closing steadily in on Henry. They rode this way for a while, slowly getting closer to each other.

Henry was the first to spot the stagecoach, and his heart nearly stopped when it got close enough to see who was driving. It definitely wasn't the normal driver, and there was only one figure sitting on the driver's bench. The other was lying on the seat. The closer he got, the more his gut churned—it was a brown-haired woman driving, and he strongly suspected it was his Opal. As he got closer, he saw her sway in the seat, even more than the natural sway of a wagon would cause. He saw her reach around the seat for something and try to reach down to the floorboards, then cry out and jerk back up. It was then he could see she was blood-soaked.

She had the reins in her hand but let the horses keep walking even as he came up beside her. Her eyes seemed out of focus.

"Opal?"

He got his horse in line with the wagon and leaned over, grasping the reins from her hands.

"Whoa, boys, whoa," he said as he gently pulled them to a halt.

He jumped down off his own horse and jumped up on the wagon bench, taking the time to set the coach brake.

"Opal!" he called out.

This time she looked up at him. "Henry?"

"Yes, darlin'," he said as he noticed streaks of blood all over her and saw the unwrapped bullet hole on her shoulder. "Where all are you hurt?"

"They're all dead. All of them." Her voice was weak.

Henry saw her pain. He felt it, too, felt the horror of so much death, but his Opal was alive. At that moment, it was all he cared about.

"Where are you hurt, Opal?"

"Shoulder and side here. It's bleeding bad on the side."

Henry looked closely and discovered it was bleeding from the front and back, so he knew the bullet went all the way through her side. He didn't see an exit wound on her shoulder so the doctor would have to dig that one out.

The deputy came up to the wagon. He saw she was in bad shape, but he had to ask, "Can you tell us what happened?"

"We were robbed, and they killed them all," she said faintly, haltingly. "There were four men I know of, maybe more. We killed one of them. They killed the man sitting with the driver. He's back there on the ground with the robber we killed. They killed the man at the horse station, too." Her chin quivered and her tears fell again. "Meredith was only fourteen. Fourteen, and they killed her."

"Hush, hush now, darlin'," Henry whispered.

By that time, Jim rode up, and shortly thereafter, Amy, in the wagon.

"Jim," Henry called out, "can you get that wagon turned around? She needs to ride back in it. I'll ride back there with her."

"Is she the only one alive?" Jim asked as he jumped down and onto the wagon to get it turned around, taking the reins from Amy.

Aaron walked his horse around to the other side of the wagon and dismounted. He opened the door and was assaulted by the smell. Holding his breath, he looked inside long enough for his eyes to adjust to the darker interior.

Suddenly, he stepped back, ran a few feet away, and vomited.

"They're all dead," he confirmed. "Three men and three women dead in there. And the driver's dead. She says two more dead on the ground back where it happened."

When he saw that the wagon was turned around, Henry called Aaron back over. "Here, take her and let me get settled in the back of the wagon, then hand her to me."

Aaron took her, taking care to jostle her as little as possible.

Sheriff Jim handed the reins back to his wife and jumped back down off the wagon. He noticed her fear and the tears in her eyes and jumped back up to hold her a minute. "Opal's going to be fine, babe. You'll see." He pulled away and looked at her reassuringly, then kissed her forehead and hopped back down to the ground.

Henry jumped up into the back of the wagon, but not so far that Aaron couldn't place Opal in his arms.

"Tie my horse to the back of the wagon, will you?" Henry asked.

"Sure thing," Aaron replied.

"Aaron," the sheriff said, "I'll drive the stage back to town. You ride on in and have Elliott at our house waiting for us." Elliott was Dr. Elliott Larkin, Jim's brother. "And better give the undertaker a heads up." He sighed. "I guess we'll have to go back and get the other three bodies in the morning."

"I'll have the doc there," Aaron said as he got up in his own saddle again and took off.

AS SOON AS Amy got the wagon underway, Jim looked with dread at the stagecoach, tied his own horse up to the back of it, and climbed up to the driver's bench. A feeling of revulsion crept over him at the thought of riding all the way back to Big Rock with the dead driver beside him and a coach full of corpses, then he reminded himself that Opal had done it, and she did it while grievously injured.

HENRY PLACED Opal so that her legs were on the wagon but her upper body was cradled in his arms. He placed tender kisses on her face, assuring her she would be fine. A couple of times, he gave her sips from the canteen and gently wiped away the drops that fell down her lips.

She moved her right hand to touch his arm and get his attention, and Henry had to lean down to hear her.

"You said you wanted me in your arms. I pictured something else."

Henry couldn't suppress the wry smile that came over his face at the irony of her humor surfacing in this tragic situation. *Oh, yes. This is my woman, all right.*

SIX

When Amy pulled the wagon in front of her house, Henry expected to see Dr. Elliott Larkin's buggy out front. He was disappointed she wouldn't get medical attention immediately, but he knew Elliott and knew he'd be there as quickly as he could.

Henry scooted to the end of the wagon, gently repositioning Opal as he moved. He picked her up and Amy led him into a guest room, hurriedly pulling down the covers so he could lay her down.

"You can go start a fire in the stove and put on a couple of big pots of water. I'll be getting her undressed," Amy said.

"You can't do that by yourself with her injuries, Amy. I'll have to help."

She considered telling him that wouldn't be proper, but she didn't argue with him. "All right. Start with her shoes and stockings. I think we'll have to cut this shirtwaist off her. I'll go get my shears. I'll go ahead and start that fire while I'm in there."

Henry didn't answer, he just nodded. His attention was focused on Opal. She'd been drifting in and out of consciousness.

He removed her short boots and stockings and set the boots on the floor in the corner, the stockings on the floor. He noticed blood on them and checked her legs to make sure she didn't have injuries there. She didn't; the blood had to be from her other wounds. Then he remembered what she'd gone through and realized the blood could have been from any of those dead bodies.

Amy came back in the room with her shears.

Henry saw them and asked, "Should we cut her out of the skirt, too, or try to turn her over so we can unbutton it?" It had always confounded Henry why so many women's fashions had closures in the back.

"I say we cut it and just pull it out from under her. I'm going to have to ruin the matching shirtwaist anyway. Besides, if I were her, I don't think I'd ever want to wear it again," Amy said.

"All right. Cut the top and skirt, but we might be able to salvage her petticoats if the ties are on the side."

Amy looked up at Henry and again decided not to question him.

"It looks like she tore the bottoms off to use for a bandage. But you're right, they could be salvaged. It wouldn't be hard to replace the ruffles."

First Amy took her shears to the petticoat bandage Opal had fashioned for the gunshot wounds on her side. She pulled it away as carefully as she could, but still, the pain finally caused Opal to pass out completely.

"Just as well," Henry said. "Let's get her out of these clothes and cleaned up before she comes back to. Maybe Elliott'll be here by then."

Together, they cut open Opal's bloody blouse down the front and cut up one sleeve and shoulder seam to free it from her arm. As she parted the front, Amy saw the cameo brooch Opal had pinned to her shift.

"That brooch must be important to her or she would have left it in her bag." Amy set the cameo on the dresser across the room.

Once Amy had cut all the way up the front of the skirt, Henry gently lifted Opal so Amy could slide the ruined clothes out from under her. He found the ties on the petticoats and unfastened them, and they were able to pull them down her legs and off her. As he did, he felt the paper bills she'd pinned to one of the petticoats.

"Smart girl. Kept some money hidden away," he said. "I think you'll have to cut her shift off her, too,"

Amy cut it up the middle and across the shoulder seams, and again, Henry gently lifted Opal just enough so Amy could pull it away. That left her in only her bloomers.

They both looked aghast at her bloody wounds but got back to their task of readying her for the doctor to be able to work on her.

Henry took the tattered shift and placed it across Opal's breasts for modesty's sake, taking care not to let it touch the shoulder wound. "Amy, if you'll get a few towels and cloths and soap, I'll get the warm water."

She nodded and rushed into the bathroom while he ran to the kitchen. They both hated to leave Opal alone, so they moved quickly. Henry returned with two large bowls and a bucket of warm water while Amy had also grabbed a clean nightgown and drawers.

Henry dropped the soap in one of the large bowls and poured warm water on top of it. He swished the soap around some, wrung out a cloth, and set himself to the task of washing Opal's face.

"There's blood in her hair, too," he said. "Once we have her all clean and ready for the doc, I'll clean her hair with a washcloth. No tellin' when she'll be able to get up and wash in the tub."

"I think she'd appreciate that, Henry. I'll be sure and tell her about the gentle care you're giving her. She might be embarrassed that you're seeing so much of her, though."

He allowed himself a small grin. "She'll have to get over it. We'll be married soon, and it won't matter anymore."

Amy washed one side of her and Henry, the other. When they encountered wounds, they cleaned up to the injury without touching it. Even her legs had smudges of blood; they wondered aloud how she had managed to get that much blood on her there. None of the possibilities they came up with were comforting. They were downright unsettling.

Amy replaced the torn, soiled shift they'd used to cover her breasts with a clean towel. They had her clean now. Mostly.

Henry untied Opal's bloomers and Amy let out a breath.

"Amy, you know we have to do this. We can see where they were wet, and we both want her clean."

"Yes. You're right. We just won't tell her you helped."

"I'll tell her. I'll do whatever it takes to take care of her."

Amy nodded at him and refreshed the washcloth and washed her. Once they had Opal washed and dried, they got the clean bloomers on her. Except for her hair and the wounds themselves, she was clean.

Just as Henry was drawing the sheet up to cover her, the front door burst open and Dr. Elliott Larkin ran in.

"Back here!" Amy called out. Henry got the dirty water and linens out of the way while Amy collected Opal's soiled and torn clothes.

"I was out at the Butler place. Mr. Butler broke his leg in two places. Good Lord," Elliott said when he saw her. "Aaron told me what happened. Ten people died, and she's the only survivor."

"Doc, it looks like one bullet went through her side, but that shoulder wound wasn't a through-and-through. Bullet's still in there," Henry said.

Elliott leaned across and palpated the skin around the shoulder wound. "I should be able to get to it easily enough; it's not very deep. Problem is this bullet probably hit a hive of tendons and vessels and nerves. I suspect it hit bone, or it probably would have gone on through. I'll have to cauterize the vessels when I get it out. The bullet being lodged in there is probably why it's not bleeding as much as the other wound."

Elliott looked at the front part of the lower wound. "Henry, can you pull her over just enough for me to see the back of it?"

Henry did.

"Doesn't look like this bullet hit any vital internal organs, so that's good. I have two main concerns we need to address. One is whether or not these wounds have material from her clothes or anything else in them. That's one of the things that causes infections. It's one of the reasons they lost so many soldiers in the war twenty years ago. I want to be extra careful to clean them out. The other thing, judging from her discarded clothes and what Aaron said, is that she's lost a lot of blood. Amy, make sure she drinks water, and try to make sure she gets down a good amount of beef broth and beef as soon as she feels like eating it. It'll help build her blood back up. It's going to take a lot of time for her to get her strength back after that much blood loss."

"All right," Amy responded.

Elliott asked Henry to go in the kitchen and bring him some of the live coals from the stove in a cast-iron skillet or pot. He'd use that to heat his instruments for the cautery.

"Henry, I'd like you to stay in here while I treat her. She's passed out now, but the intense pain may rouse her. I'll need you to hold her, so she doesn't jerk, especially when I probe for that bullet. I don't have any surgical anesthetic. Just laudanum for later."

"All right."

THE PROCEDURES WERE COMPLETED, and Elliott called everyone together in the parlor after he washed up. By this time, Jim had returned from the undertaker.

"She'll most likely sleep through the night. If she wakes, it's all right if she drinks water or broth. I'd leave a candle lit or a lantern turned down low, in case she wakes up disoriented."

"I'm staying here," Henry said. "I'm sorry to invite myself, but I'm not leaving. I'll sleep in a chair by her bed. She's not going to be alone."

Jim understood. "We'll move a comfortable chair in there for you."

Henry nodded gratefully.

"I expect she'll come out with no more than a few scars. I'm going to visit a couple of times a day and keep an eye out for any signs of infection. She's going to need a while to heal up."

"We'll take care of her," Amy said.

"There's something else I want to mention about her healing. Physically, I think she'll be fine, eventually. But emotionally, I can't predict what might happen. She saw ten people die today and struggled hard to keep herself alive. In a few hours, she lived more horrors than most people see in a lifetime. I've heard stories of men in the war who witnessed that kind of carnage and never got over it. She might be willing to talk about it; she might refuse to and want to ignore it. I hope she'll talk about it, because I think that'll help her deal with it. I can't imagine being able to just forget something like that happened."

"Maybe she'll talk to us," Henry said. "When I first got to

her, she cried because they killed a fourteen year old girl. She was able to tell us a little bit about what happened."

"Good. That's a good start. Don't pressure her, but let her know you're there to listen. She might want to talk to the reverend, too, if she's a religious woman. He might be able to offer her some comfort. Take your cues from her. If she's of a mind to talk about what she's feeling, then listen. Sometimes in a situation like this, survivors feel guilty that they survived. It's a hard thing to get over."

Elliott promised to come back first thing in the morning. Jim and Henry moved a comfortable upholstered chair and ottoman into Opal's room and Henry settled in for the night. He wouldn't leave her side to eat supper, so Amy brought him a plate of food.

NO ONE SLEPT MUCH, and Amy was up well before dawn making coffee. Jim was already in the kitchen when Henry made his way in.

Amy spoke first as she poured a cup for each of the men. "I need to send a wire to her brother Ben and let him know what happened. I'm sure Caleb's already working on a news article about it, and I don't want Ben to find out by reading it in the paper."

"I talked to Caleb last night," Jim said. "Asked him to wait until after we get the bodies today and after we have a chance to find out more information from Opal. He won't put it over the wire until this afternoon. We don't have much to go on until we can talk to her. I'll be going through the passenger's personal things today to see what we can find out there. But, yes, Ben should know she's alive and the outlook is good."

Amy started breakfast and made a big batch of biscuits so

there would be leftovers. She sliced ham and fried it, then scrambled eggs.

"Mighty good food, Amy. I appreciate it," Henry said.

Amy smiled and put her hand on his arm. "Today was supposed to be your wedding day. I'm so sorry things turned out the way they did."

Henry gave her a rueful smile. "I got no right to complain much. Opal's alive when so many others died. She should make it just fine, so I ought to count myself blessed. Waiting for the wedding is a small thing."

"Well," Jim said, "if she's lucid when she wakes up today, no reason we can't go ahead and get Reverend Copperfield over here."

"Oh, Jim, I expect she'll be far too sore to think about marriage today. Elliott left the laudanum for that, you know." Amy scowled at him.

"All right, I'm just saying you don't have to wait until she's fully healed if you don't want to. You'll have to wait for the honeymoon, but you don't have to wait for the vows."

Henry considered that and nodded.

Shortly after daybreak, Deputy Aaron Glover showed up. Amy poured him a cup of coffee.

"Jeb didn't have enough caskets for everybody last night, but he got the ladies taken care of," Aaron said. "Angus volunteered the men up at the sawmill to make the rest of the caskets. The stagecoach is still at the livery. We need to get a good look at it and check out the baggage and see what we might learn from it. It's going to need a powerful amount of cleaning if the stage company plans to use it again. They'll probably have to replace the seats—too many bullet holes and too much blood."

"We'll have to get right on all that this afternoon. We'd probably do best to get Deacon and Reed to help us locate families of the victims. I know Will at the stage office wired the stage line offices last night. Word's going to be all over town real soon," Jim said.

Deacon Snow and his brother, Reed, were private detectives in town who had previously worked with the sheriff's office on several cases.

"Jim, why don't you stay here and get started on all that this morning? Can't help but think one of us should stay here in town. I can get another one of the men to go with me to get those three bodies," Aaron said.

Jim sighed. "I guess that would be more practical. You can take my wagon. Probably will be a lot going on around here. We need to identify those bodies. I sure hope Opal will feel like talking to us today. All we know is that one of the couples is kin to Clint. I didn't let him see the bodies in the stage. A man shouldn't have to see a loved one like that."

There was a soft knock on the front door, then it opened, and Elliott walked in. Amy poured him the last of the coffee and made another pot.

"Is she still out?" he asked.

"She was as of about ten minutes ago."

"I'll go look in on her," Elliott said as he set his coffee cup down.

Soon he came back in and joined them at the table.

"Do you think she'll be able to answer questions when she wakes up?"

"She should, most likely," Elliott said. "She'll be sore, especially considering what she must have put her body through to get here, even on top of the gunshot wounds. But when she first wakes up I expect she'll be able to talk. When she complains of pain, though, I'll give her laudanum." He looked at Amy. "Mind if I have a couple of those biscuits?"

She stood and smiled at him. "You want gravy or butter and preserves?"

"Gravy. Oh, I meant to remind you, don't give her any willow bark tea for pain. It might make her bleed more. She can have anything else she wants, though."

When he was finished with his breakfast, Henry excused himself to go sit with Opal again. A few minutes later, Elliott joined him. They heard the front door close and figured Jim had left. That was confirmed when Amy walked in.

Elliott was satisfied when he saw that the wounds weren't bleeding through the bandages. As he began pulling the one off her side so he could look under it, Opal stirred.

"Opal?" Both Amy and Henry called her name.

Her eyes fluttered open and the pain hit her when she moved. "Oh!" She squeezed her eyes shut in reaction. Amy ran out to see if she could catch Jim in time so he could try to get information from Opal.

"You were injured by gunfire, Opal, in the shoulder and your side," Elliott said. "You're in Amy's house. I'm Elliott, your doctor. And of course, Henry's here. He hasn't left your side all night."

She slowly opened her eyes again and looked at each of them, her eyes taking a little longer to focus than they normally would.

"Try not to move unless you have to; you don't want to start up the bleeding again. I know it hurts now, but you should heal up just fine. Can you tell me how you feel?"

Her voice still sounded weak and groggy from sleep. "Like I got shot. First time it's happened to me. I don't like it."

Henry and Elliott both smiled at her. "I don't like it, either, darlin'," Henry said.

"Is it all right if I drink some water?"

"Yes," Henry said as he jumped up from his chair to pour a small amount into a cup. He held it to her lips as she sipped. "Easy, darlin'."

Jim and Amy entered.

"Opal?" Jim asked. "I'm Jim, Amy's husband. Can you answer some questions for us?"

"I'll try."

Jim took some paper out of his pocket.

"Do you know the names of the people on the stagecoach with you?"

"The Deans and their daughter, Meredith. I don't know their Christian names. The Tatums—they were visiting people here in town. Mrs. Tatum had on a yellow dress and he wore spectacles. And Mr. Keppler. He was the one who shot Red Eye."

"This is helpful, Opal. Can you tell us anything about the robbers? You said one was called Red Eye. What about the others?"

"There was one named Jed. The one giving orders—I think they called him Malachi—he had an accent. English. And a Herman, somebody named Herman. I must have passed out. I'm not sure how long I was out. Then it took me forever to get out of the coach and up on top to drive it. That's all I can remember. Oh, I remember seeing Mr. Birdwhistle dead."

"Mr. Birdwhistle?" Jim asked.

"The man at the horse station at Williston. He was already dead when I got there. That's what Keppler said his name was, if it's the same man who's been there before. They must have killed him first before they hit the stage."

"All right, we've got Malachi, Red Eye, Herman, and Jed. Do you know how many there were?"

"I only saw two of them, Red Eye and Jed. I heard four. There could have been more. I just don't know."

"Thank you, Opal, I'll let you rest now," Jim said. He nodded to the others in the room and left again.

"I need to go to the bathroom, Amy," Opal said.

"I don't want you exerting, Opal. We need to be careful about bleeding," Elliott said. "Henry or I will carry you in there, and Amy can help you."

Opal whimpered a complaint.

"I'll carry you, darlin'," Henry said. "Amy can help you, and I'll carry you back. Now that Elliott's already examined you, we can get that gown on you."

Opal then realized how close to naked she was.

Henry lifted her into a sitting position while Opal held the sheet to her body. Amy got the nightgown and pulled it over her head. She had chosen a very loose one that buttoned down the front, but it was full enough that it went over her head even when buttoned. Amy had reasoned that Elliott might be able to check her wounds later just by unbuttoning part of it rather than having to remove it.

They accomplished the trip to the bathroom with no complications, but Opal felt embarrassed even though Henry left the room while she did her business. When he set her back down on the bed, she realized how much the exertion took out of her.

"How's your pain now?" Elliott asked.

"It hurts. Before I went in there, it mainly hurt when I moved. Now it hurts sitting still."

Elliott pulled out a spoon and gave her some laudanum. "This will help you sleep. I need you to be as still as you can for a day or two. Amy's going to fix you some beef broth, and I want you to drink it. It'll help make you strong again. If you feel like eating, tell Amy. There's no reason you can't. But right now, the first order of business is to rest and try not to move much."

She made a face at the taste, and Henry was quick with the cup of water to help wash the taste away.

"Thank you both," Opal said. Henry gently laid her back so

she didn't have to flex her muscles and reawaken pain in her side.

SHE SLEPT ALL DAY. Amy persuaded Henry to go home for a while and get a change of clothes and tend to his animals. She let him know he was welcome to continue staying during the nights.

The Ladies' Aid Society learned of the situation and wanted to do its part to help Amy take care of one of their brides. Before lunchtime, there was a knock at the door and four ladies from the group came in with arms full of food. They all wanted to look in on Opal, and Amy let them peek as long as they didn't make noise.

When Jim came home for lunch, he brought Opal's bags and trunk from the coach. He said when Aaron picked up the bodies, the ladies' handbags were still on the ground. The murderers had apparently taken the men's wallets and jewelry but left the reticules. Her valise was found opened on the floor of the coach. It still held some jerky snacks, paper, pencils, a book, and her journal. He asked Amy to try to remove as much of the blood from the items as she could before giving them to Opal.

Aaron had recognized the man riding shotgun from previous stage rides, but none of them remembered his name. The driver, they all knew as Charley Sutton. Opal had said the man at the way station was named Birdwhistle and they operated under that assumption.

Amy spent quite a bit of time choosing the right words for the wire to Ben. She finally settled on mainly assuring him Opal was all right and being taken care of.

. . .

STAGE ATTACKED north of here STOP Several fatalities STOP Opal injured STOP Is recuperating will be fine STOP Wedding is postponed STOP Amy Larkin

---

OPAL WOKE up sore the next morning. Not only were her wounds sore, but her muscles were sore from her exertion of merely trying to survive. The loss of blood caused her a good deal of weakness, too. She felt good enough to drink plenty of broth, though, and she ate some eggs and bacon for breakfast.

Henry stayed with her. He fed her even though she insisted she could feed herself. She had to let him hold her cup when she took a drink, but that was mainly because the cup was on the bedside table and out of her reach.

"I surely do wish things had happened more according to our plans," she said to him.

"Me, too, sweetheart, but we'll still get married. Just not as quickly as I wanted to. At least I still get to spend time with you," Henry said as he took her hand.

"I'm glad you're here. When do you think we can marry?"

"Jim reminded me we can exchange vows whenever you feel like it. You haven't healed enough for a true wedding night, but we can postpone that part."

Opal was a little embarrassed at hearing him refer to their sexual relationship. She looked up at him again. "I'm sorry you have to wait for that part."

Henry smiled broadly at her, almost laughing. "I'm not the only one of us who has to wait." He leaned down to be sure Amy wouldn't overhear him from the other room. "I promise I'll make it as pleasurable for you as I possibly can. I think you'll enjoy it, too."

Opal smiled tentatively, not sure what to say or how to react.

Before long, Elliott popped in to check on his patient. "How are you feeling, Opal?"

"Sore. But I feel marginally better than yesterday."

"Well, I like hearing that! Is it all right if I take a look? I'd like to change the bandages and redress the wounds."

"Of course."

Elliott unbuttoned only enough buttons to pull the gown over and reveal her shoulder. Henry held the gown out of the way while Elliott removed the bandage. He told them it looked as good as he hoped, and he redressed it then buttoned her gown back up. Then he unbuttoned some lower buttons and positioned the gown, so her side was accessible.

"Henry, I don't want her putting weight on that shoulder or flexing. Would you lift her up so I can get to the backside of this bullet hole?"

Henry sat on the bed beside Opal, facing her. He leaned over and lifted her by putting one arm behind her head, resting that hand on her shoulder blade. The other arm went around her just above the injury. He hugged her tightly to him, lifting her so no pressure was placed on her shoulder and she didn't have to exert to stay in place.

Elliott was happy with that one, too, and shared his thoughts. "It looks like you're going to heal nicely, Opal. I'm glad to see no signs of infection. Heaven knows you've got two attentive caregivers in Henry and Amy."

"I'm glad, too. They're taking very good care of me," Opal said.

"How's the pain now that I've moved you around some?"

"It's sore. Still better than yesterday, though."

"It will be for a few days, but it should be a little better each day. I want you to keep eating and drinking as much as you want. You need to build your blood back up."

"I will. This one," she pointed at Henry, "doesn't give me a choice."

"Doc, I wanted to ask you about how long you expect it to take for her to get healed up."

Elliott knew their situation and that they had planned to marry the day after she arrived.

"Henry, is this about the wedding? Are you asking me how soon it'll be before it's safe to have marital relations?"

Opal went red.

"Yes, I am," Henry asserted.

"I'd like to see her heal for about four or five weeks, and even then, you need to keep it on the tame side. Another week or two after that before you get overly energetic and acrobatic."

Opal groaned in embarrassment and lowered her head. The men both grinned quickly then recovered their composure.

"All right," Henry said. "We were thinking about going ahead with the vows, though, and just waiting for the honeymoon. At some point in the next couple of weeks or so, I'd like to get married and move her to our house."

"That shouldn't be a problem. She'll be feeling much better by then." Elliott repacked his supplies and picked up his medical bag. "I'll see you folks this evening."

After he left, Opal asked him to call Amy in to help her to the bathroom.

"I can help you in there. Elliott said it's all right to walk if you can. I'll just put my arm around you in case you get too weak."

"Amy can do that."

He looked at her the way he might look at a misbehaving child. "Really? Amy can pick you up and carry you if you falter?"

"Oh, all right. Just take me in there, and I can do the rest myself."

"All right. Let's give it a try. Want me to call Amy just in case?"

"No, not yet. I'll yell if I need her."

Henry pulled her up and helped her sit on the side of the bed. He helped her stand and held her arm while she steadied herself. When she took a small step, he put his arm loosely around her waist and held his other arm out so she could use it to steady herself.

She gave him a glowing smile when she made it into the bathroom and over to the chamber pot chair.

"You can leave now. I think I've got this."

"Call out if you need one of us."

Opal took care of it by herself and was able to stand by holding on to a table. She steadied herself that way as she walked over to the bowl and pitcher and washed her hands and face.

She opened the door and beamed a smile at Henry. "I think I'd like to sit at the table for a few minutes."

"Sure, sweetheart. I still want to steady you, though."

She looked at him indulgently. "I don't need it, but all right. I like having you close by."

Opal sat at the kitchen table and watched Amy scramble eggs for her and Henry. She had already cooked biscuits and bacon earlier, but she'd waited to cook their eggs until Opal was ready to eat.

"I wish I could help you, Am. I hate that you're having to wait on me like this," Opal said, lapsing readily into their youthful habit of calling each other by the first syllable of their names.

"Op, there's nothing I'd rather do. This isn't the reunion I planned, either, but I'm thrilled to have you here. I just wish you weren't in pain. I hate that part!"

A shadow crossed Opal's face. "I know, but I don't feel I have a right to complain. It could have been so much worse."

Amy set a cup of coffee in front of Opal, cream and sugar already in it; she remembered how her friend liked it. She joined them at the table after she placed their plates in front of them. Henry took the hand that Opal wasn't supposed to use yet and held it.

"It must have been awful, Op. My heart breaks when I think of what you went through."

Opal picked up her fork. "Those poor people. And Meredith only fourteen years old. It was just so senseless. How people can do that to other people is just beyond me. She was just a child." Opal's eyes filled with tears.

"I wish I had an explanation for you, sweetheart," Henry said. "I wish to goodness it hadn't happened. I tell myself I should have met you in Rawlins, and we could have been married there. Or I could have met you there and ridden back with you, maybe I could have changed the outcome some."

She smiled at him. "You might have been killed, too, then where would I be? No, I know it does no good to dwell on the what-ifs. I don't want you to torture yourself that way. It happened. I don't know how it fits into God's plan, but I believe things happen for a reason. I just can't imagine what the reason could possibly be for this. We may not understand until we get to Heaven."

"I was in there when you told Jim about the men and the victims. What about you, Opal? I've been wanting to ask you how you managed to survive," Henry asked.

Opal took a deep breath. "I remember we were having a nice conversation, and I was eager to arrive at my new home that day.

The man riding shotgun knocked on the coach and told us to get guns if we had them. I saw Mr. Keppler get his. I remember being so scared, just like the other women. I remember a man appeared at the door with a rifle and demanded our valuables. There was another man near the door, too, but I didn't see his face, just his gun hand. There were voices outside." She stopped. "It gets all jumbled then, and I must have passed out at some point because when I came to, the bodies of two men were on top of me. I was injured and had a hard time breathing. I don't know how long I was out. I just knew I was the only one alive." She closed her eyes, scrunching them as if to rid herself of the image in her head.

"You don't have to talk about it if you don't want to," Amy said softly.

"I'm all right," she continued. She seemed to stare at her plate. "I remember having trouble getting the bodies off me. I didn't know how weak and shaky I was until I tried to stand and couldn't. But I managed. I managed to get across the coach to the door, then I had to figure out how to get down without passing out from the pain. I had to drop down on my bottom and get down a little at a time, and it hurt. I had to lean on the coach to stand and move inches at a time. I had to step on the dead man because I didn't think I could walk all the way around his body without holding on to something. The body of the man who rode shotgun was under the wheel, so I had to get the horses to back up so I could get him out of the way."

"Oh, sweetheart," Henry said.

She smiled ruefully at him and continued. "The part that took the most out of me was getting up to that driver's seat. It looked like it must have been forty feet off the ground. Felt like it, too. Took me forever, climbing up the wagon wheel and pulling up. That's when my side started to bleed a lot. When I finally managed to get up there, I was on the body of the driver. I think I told him I was sorry."

Henry took her hand in both of his.

"So that's when I saw so much blood on me and wrapped my side. I think you know the rest."

They didn't speak for a few minutes. Opal drank her coffee; it had cooled just enough to allow her to down nearly the whole cup at once. She took a deep breath and pulled apart her biscuit to put butter on it while Amy refilled her cup.

———

HENRY HELPED her back to her bed. "How is your pain? Elliott said we could give you laudanum if it's really bad."

"It hurts, but I'd rather save that for nighttime if I can. Let me just try to relax. It's not that bad when I'm still. I have an idea. Why don't you read to me?"

Henry smiled. "All right. I saw a book I like in the parlor. I'll go get it."

When he came back in, he set the book down while he helped Opal get into a comfortable position for sleep. Then he sat down, picked up the book, and started reading *The Adventures of Tom Sawyer*.

She fell asleep with a small smile on her face, and Henry went back to the kitchen to talk to Amy.

"Amy, I told Elliott I want to marry Opal and take her to our house in a week or two, and he said that should be all right. You've taken such good care of both of us and I appreciate it more than you can know. But she'll be to the point where I can take care of her, and I'd like to do that in our home."

She sighed then smiled. "I can understand that. Elliott said it'll take time to rebuild her strength, so I imagine we should keep the ceremony small and private. We can have it here, if that's all right with you."

"Of course! I want Angus and Nessa here. He'll be my best

man. Then just you two and us and the reverend and his wife; that should be it."

"It'll be nice to concentrate on something happy. When she was telling us what she went through this morning, I nearly broke down."

"Me, too. I hope her being able to talk about it will help her get beyond the horror of it."

Amy felt compelled to say something. "You know, she was right when she said you shouldn't think about what you could have done to prevent it happening. You'll only make yourself and Opal miserable if you think that way. The best thing you can do is show her what she has to live for, to be happy for."

Henry gave her a quick hug. "I can do that."

"And you might as well get used to this, too; I'll be coming over to visit often until she's all healed."

"Wouldn't have it any other way," he said on his way out the door. "I'm going home to clean up, and then I'll be back."

HENRY ARRIVED BACK at the same time Jim came home for lunch.

"Caleb stopped by the jail on his way here to bring this wire to Opal," Jim said, handing Henry the envelope. "I told him I'd bring it. He said it's good news."

Henry opened the envelope and read the message.

BENJAMIN DALE MCALLISTER, Jr. born Tuesday STOP 7 pounds STOP Mother and baby fine STOP Hope you are getting well STOP Please write STOP Ben M

. . .

"OH, she'll be happy to hear this. She's been wondering about Zora and the baby. I'd better get a pen and paper from Amy because she's going to want to write that letter now."

Opal was still asleep, so the rest of them settled down for lunch. As they passed their plates, Henry asked how the effort to find the killers was going and if they'd been able to notify the families of the dead.

Jim shook his head and ran his fingers through his hair in apparent frustration. "Well, we know from Clint that the Tatums don't have any family. We're going to bury them here. Clint's in contact with a lawyer about the disposition of their property and assets. I think he's looking to donate them to a worthy cause the Tatums would have supported."

"That's a nice thing," Amy said. "Since Caleb published that news story, I've been surprised people haven't been like vultures trying to get their hands on it."

"The story hasn't been out long. It'll happen, I'm sure. My worry is that he let people know there was a survivor on her way to marry. I convinced him not to mention she would live here. Problem is there aren't that many places she could have been headed to on that stage. They're bound to figure it out. We don't need those killers in town, planning to make sure Opal can't identify them." He purposefully avoided saying "... planning to kill her..." for Henry's sake, but Henry knew what he meant.

"I've been worried about that, too. What do you know about the killers?"

"Malachi is most likely Malachi Stone, according to the police in Rawlins. He's slippery. They haven't been able to capture him, haven't ever even seen him. They only know he has an accent and he's damn good at what he does. He came over here from England, and word is he was running from the law then. Red Eye, the one Keppler shot, was Redmond 'Red Eye' Gilbert, another low-life who's been with Stone for a while.

We're still trying to figure out who Jed and Herman are. They must be fairly new to Stone's gang. The Snows are working on it."

"They don't know where any of them live?"

"Could be anywhere in all these mountains. They think Red Eye had some family up near Sioux territory. Really, they could be anywhere in the damn territory. It's too easy to disappear in this country. We don't think Stone's married. No idea about Jed or Herman."

"Will there be a funeral for the Tatums?" Amy asked.

"Yes, day after tomorrow," Jim said.

Amy looked at Henry. "Opal will want to go. We need to be sure to ask Elliott."

SEVEN

The town of Big Rock felt the gruesomeness of the stagecoach massacre. All were horrified and of one mind in wanting to support Opal and help her get past this awful thing. They were also of one mind in wanting the perpetrators to face the consequences.

It was possible that Harriet felt the most outraged and also the most helplessly responsible. Opal was one of their mail order brides, after all. If not for her efforts in getting Opal there, she never would have suffered such a harrowing experience.

Harriet continued to arrange for the Ladies' Aid Society to provide foods occasionally and to come sit and visit when Opal felt like it. The women who visited all agreed that Opal was a warm and friendly person, exactly the kind of woman they hoped found happiness in a Big Rock marriage. She fit right in.

The funeral for the Tatums was attended by most of the town, including Opal, who had put on a dress for the first time since she arrived. Henry was very attentive and solicitous of her, but wasn't able to console her when her tears started to fall. She wept quietly. Reverend Copperfield didn't mention the robbery and murders specifically, and Henry was grateful Opal didn't have to hear them mentioned. Her own memories were bad enough. Instead, the reverend shared information about the Tatums that Clint Keller had provided and preached about the comfort Clint had from knowing his sister and brother-in-law were in the arms of God now.

After the service, Henry whisked Opal away quickly and quietly; Jim and Amy lingered to visit with the other townspeople. He got her back to the Larkins' house and helped her undress and put her gown on again. Opal no longer felt any embarrassment over him seeing her body. In her mind, in that specific regard, they were as good as married already. He'd already seen her so many times.

"Can I get you something to drink, sweetie?"

"I could use a sip of brandy, I think."

He smiled at her. "I saw a bottle on Jim's bookshelf. Be right back." In just a few minutes, he returned with a snifter and the bottle.

"Really, just a sip or two, I think," Opal said.

Henry poured a small amount and handed it to her. "I didn't know you drink brandy."

"I never have before, but I know people drink it when awful things happen and they need something bracing."

"They do. I recommend very small sips. It's sweet and fruity, but it's mighty strong and packs a punch."

"All right."

Opal touched her lips to the amber liquid, then tasted them.

"Uhhh..." she groaned. "Is this an acquired taste?"

Henry chuckled. "Yes, it is. Take a tiny sip. It gets better. I'm sure you need it after that funeral."

"It hit me so hard again that I survived. So many died, but I survived. That's hard to think about. Hard to live with."

"Would it be better if you had died, too?"

She looked at him. "What?"

"Imagine you had died, too, sweetheart."

She took another sip.

"I guess you'd be mourning me. And Ben and Zora, and Amy would be mourning, too."

"Yes, we would. I'd have been heartbroken, Opal. Is there anything that would be better if you had died that day?"

"I hadn't looked at it like that. I wouldn't have ever met you. I wouldn't have seen Amy. My brother and sister-in-law would be crushed." She looked away in thought. "No, nothing would have been better."

"No, and there wouldn't have been anyone left alive to tell us about the criminals. The authorities might never have figured out who committed the crimes. It's very possible they would have gotten away with it. Now, since you were able to give them information, Jim and the other authorities have a good chance of tracking them down and bringing them to justice."

She sighed. "I know you're right. I do. Thank you for reminding me of those things. The memories still hurt, though." She sipped some more brandy.

"I hope they fade with time, sweetie. I'll do everything I can to help you leave them in the past. Maybe the best way to honor the ones who've gone is to help bring their killers to justice, and to live your own life looking forward, as they didn't get to do."

She smiled at him. "Do you know how much I love you, Henry?"

It was the first time she'd said those words.

"Probably not as much as I love you."

A FEW DAYS PASSED, and Elliott wanted Opal to begin moving her arm and side more. He showed her and Henry how to do the motions and stretches she needed to do to ease back into her full range of motion. They made her uncomfortable at first, but Elliott insisted that she push herself just a little, and the sooner she did it, the sooner she would feel like her old self.

It wasn't long before Opal's skin wounds healed over well, with some expected scarring. The internal injuries were taking longer but were expected to heal right on track. She could use her arm, but Elliott advised her not to lift much with it. She was more aware of her side injuries because she felt the internal wound with nearly every move—getting up, getting down, leaning over, turning, stooping, just about everything a person does when not sitting or lying still. It wasn't pain exactly that she felt, just an uncomfortable reminder that she hadn't fully healed yet.

The day finally came for their wedding. It was a crisp, sunny Saturday and the ceremony was scheduled for noon. They planned to say their vows, eat lunch with the wedding party, and then move Opal to Henry's house. *Their* house.

It was a simple ceremony. Opal looked lovely in her new wedding dress. She had her mother's embroidered handkerchief as something old, she wore the dress and hair comb as two somethings new, she pinned the cameo brooch on her dress for something blue, and Amy let her borrow a thin gold bracelet. The only ones in attendance were Opal and Henry, Jim and Amy, Angus and Nessa, and the Reverend and Mrs. Copperfield.

The following luncheon was low key but celebratory. No one seemed to want to mention the purpose for the delay; conversation was positive and forward-looking.

"I reckon the Ladies' Aid Society is working on their next mail order bride. Looks like they've had two successes thus far," Angus said as he winked at his wife Nessa, the society's first mail order bride.

Amy laughed. "They're looking at the next two right now. Harriet is enjoying playing matchmaker. She's trying her best to find out everything about the women and everything about the men so she can absolutely make the most perfect matches."

"I can believe that," Henry said as he smiled, raising an eyebrow. "I was surprised at some of the things she talked to me about."

Angus chuckled as he swirled his drink in his glass. "I ken what ye mean. I was surprised at just how *frank* she was wi' me, too."

"What do you mean?" Nessa asked.

Angus looked around the table and shrugged. "All right, we're all married couples here now. Let's just say she was curious about how often I expected to have relations in my marriage."

Mrs. Copperfield looked stunned.

"Why, she didn't ask me any such thing," Nessa said.

"Me, either!" Opal exclaimed.

Jim let out a deep belly laugh. "You'll get used to Harriet. Suffice it to say, we've come to suspect that her appetites are... more than most, stronger than most."

Amy smirked but didn't say anything. She knew Harriet's secrets.

"Darker than most. And she must think of it all the time," Angus said as he laughed with him. "Along those lines, Henry, my mate, ye and Opal can expect a visit from Harriet and Arthur in a few days. She'll have a welcoming gift for ye." He winked at Nessa.

"That sounds lovely," Opal said.

"You'll be surprised, I'm sure," Nessa said with a big smile on her face.

"So, Angus," Jim said, curious and amused, "what did you tell Harriet about how often you expect to enjoy the pleasures of marriage?"

"Well, after I picked my jaw up off the floor, I told her I planned to stop once in a while to eat."

The men cackled, and Nessa joined them, shaking her head as she laughed. "Trust me. He doesn't eat nearly as often as you'd think such a giant of a man should."

"I'm a man o' priorities." Angus shrugged with a grin.

The conversation died down as everyone finished their dessert and after-dinner coffee. The men offered to help Henry with Opal's bags and trunk. Opal returned the borrowed bracelet to Amy and they hugged, making tentative plans to get together mid-week for a visit. They invited Nessa and Mrs. Copperfield to join them if they were available.

Before long, Henry lifted Opal up onto the seat of the wagon and they were on their way. It only took a few minutes to get to their house.

"I'm so glad we live this close to Amy and Jim. It's going to be a blessing to be able to visit her after being apart for so many years," Opal said.

"I'm happy for you, sweetheart. It's wonderful you already have a good friend here."

"In a day or two, will you take me around town, show it to me?"

"Yes, ma'am, of course I will. How about Monday, we go to Miz Mary's restaurant for breakfast then go to the mercantile for supplies and groceries?"

"Yes! But shouldn't you go to work on Monday?"

"No, Angus has been holding the fort down for me all this time. They won't be expecting me back for a few days yet, not when we just got married."

A look of concern came over her face. "I'm sorry it won't be the wedding night you hoped for. I promise I'll do everything I can to make it—"

He cut her off. "Opal, tonight, I'll have you in bed beside me.

Maybe you'll go to sleep in my arms. That's the best night I could have."

Just then Henry pulled up in front of a two-story, white clapboard house with green shutters.

Opal's eyes widened as she took in the big house with a huge yard and the big white fence enclosing it all. "Henry, it's so beautiful! I wasn't expecting this."

"I'm glad you like your new home. I have the daughter of a co-worker who comes in and cleans, and sometimes she cooks for me, too. She's helped me make it into a place that might be fit for a woman. Before I hired her," he said, laughing, "it was only pretty on the outside. Now the inside's nice enough for me, but I'm sure you'll want to make it yours, you know, change things around and make it into something you like. Add the furniture you like. I told you I don't have much in there, mainly necessities."

He climbed down to the ground, turned, then held out his arms for her. Instead of putting her on the ground, he carried her up the four steps, across the porch, and into the house.

Once inside, he set her down and pulled her into a kiss. "Welcome home, Mrs. Tucker. I sure do hope you like it."

She gave him a sly glance and a mischievous grin. "Well, it helps that you're here."

He chuckled. "And Amy's close, too, so you won't have to run far if you decide you need to escape."

"That is a consoling thought," she teased. Her eyes wandered around, taking in her new home. They stopped when she saw a huge, beautiful double bookcase that dominated most of one wall of the parlor. It had a big fabric bow tied around the upper left corner.

"Henry, what a beautiful bookcase! Is... is that... did you make that for me?"

Her obvious joy made him feel like a king. "I did. Your

name's inscribed on the upper side molding piece. I got Angus to help me with that part—he's a master at carved scrollwork detail."

She hurried over to look at it, removing the bow so she could see her name. She reached up to run her fingers over the detailing. It was the first time she'd seen her married name written out, *Opal Tucker*.

Opal turned to her husband, tiptoed and kissed him again, pushing her body into his. Her passion ignited his, and she put her hand on his increasing length.

"Opal, we need to be careful. You know what Elliott said."

"Are you going to listen to Elliott or your wife?"

"Do you have any idea what you're saying?"

"I have an idea. Lots of ideas. Even if we can't, you know, I think there are things we *can* do."

He pulled her into another more passionate kiss. "I do believe Harriet knew what she was doing in pairing you with me. I need to send that woman some flowers and chocolates."

Henry surprised her by picking her up again. She let out a little yelp. "What are you doing?"

"I'm getting you acquainted with the bedroom." By then, they were in the bedroom and he put her down. He knelt and removed her shoes and stockings, not particularly gently, and she had to put her hands on his shoulders to steady herself. He kicked off his own boots and quickly pulled off his thick socks. His jacket landed on the floor on top of the boots.

Opal stood on tiptoe again to kiss him. She pushed herself against him and moaned when she felt his reaction. She turned her back to him. "Will you unbutton me?"

"Opal, I'm afraid we might go too far."

"Let me remind you that you've been undressing me since the day I got here. And doing very intimate things for me."

"I was taking care of you—that's different than this," he said as he undid the buttons and pulled off her shirtwaist. Before she could turn back around, he pulled the decorative comb and the pins from her hair and fluffed it out loosely over her shoulders and down her back.

"Yes. That was *very* different than this." Opal unbuttoned her skirt and let it fall, then she untied her petticoat and let it fall, too. She wore only one. Left in her bloomers and shift, she tiptoed again to kiss Henry. She unbuttoned his shirt and the placket of his pants.

"Opal," Henry whispered as he caressed her breasts through the thin cotton of her shift. "You shouldn't be—"

"Yes, I should." Opal slowly slid to one knee, then both. She looked up at him as she reached into the opening of his britches and opened his drawers and pulled them down and off him.

Henry's breath caught when she took his length into her hands, and he moaned when her lips touched him there. "You don't have to do this," he said.

"No, I don't," Opal responded. "But I want to. You'll have to tell me if I'm doing it poorly. Or tell me how you want me to do it."

His hands found her hair and stroked it, finally taking most of it and twirling it into one hand, away from her face so he could see more clearly. "Yes, just like that," he whispered hoarsely as her tongue teased and flicked all down the shaft, darting back to the sac and licking there, too. He moaned again.

Her tongue came back to the mushroom head, lapped around it, then flicked it all around before encircling it with her mouth and gently sucking. As she sucked, she continued the gentle manipulation of her tongue.

"Opal, honey, if you aren't careful, I'll spend in your mouth." She looked up at him and redoubled her efforts, letting him know that's what she wanted.

Henry made a guttural sound much like a growl. "Then suck a little harder, darlin', it won't take much more."

Opal felt him pull her hair and didn't know if it was intentional or not, then she decided it was, when she felt him subtly try to control her head movements. She felt him push a little more into her mouth and urge her into faster movements.

She saw him throw his head back with a low bellow and felt his release accumulate on the back of her tongue. She swallowed two or three times to get it all down.

Opal finished by sweetly licking and sucking him clean before she pulled away.

"Sweet Lord, woman, you've got me weak in the knees. I never expected that." He chuckled as he sat on the side of the bed and pulled her up to sit beside him. "I didn't expect you'd even know about that."

It was Opal's turn to laugh. "Most of my friends back home are married. And I lived with my sister-in-law, remember. We talked."

"Opal, that was, that was wonderful. I don't even know what to say. I could say I love you. I could say thank you. I could say *damn*, that was fine. All would be true."

"Then I take it I did it well enough. I was a little worried it wouldn't be exactly how you'd like it."

"Oh, my sweet wife." Henry laughed as he took her into his arms, being careful with her shoulder. "I can't imagine how it could possibly have been any better. You took my breath away. Now let me rest and catch my breath, and I want to make you feel that good, too."

"Henry, I didn't do that for the sake of reciprocity. I wanted you to have some satisfaction on your wedding night."

"I told you I'd have been happy just to have you beside me in our bed, but I'm sure as hell not going to argue with your plan," he said as he laughed, then he grew more serious. "And now, little one, I want more than ever to climb between your legs and sample the treats that wait for me there. Let's get the rest of these clothes off," he said as he pulled the shift over her head and untied her bloomers. He still wore his unbuttoned shirt, so he threw it off, too.

Henry pulled the covers out of the way and guided Opal onto the bed diagonally, so he'd have more room. With his mouth and free hand, he teased her nipples without mercy until she purred and begged for more. He kissed a trail down her belly until he came to her curls, then he kissed lower. Henry let his hand wander her inner thighs and cleft, thrilled to find them bathed in her wetness. He spread her legs more, enough to accommodate him, and lowered his head to her bud.

Opal gasped and moaned when she felt his tongue at her opening. He licked all around it and just inside, then inserted a finger.

"I can hardly wait until I can plunge inside you and feel your wet warmth around me."

"Then do it, Henry, please. I want you so much right now!"

He quickened the pace of his finger, then he inserted two.

"You know we can't yet. I don't want to hurt you. The way I feel right now, I can't promise I'll be gentle. Let me just do this for you for now."

His tongue went back to her little pearl as the thrusts of his fingers were met by her own movements. He curled his fingers inside her as he sucked her nub, and she called out as her back arched and her legs clamped around him. The arching movement reminded her that her side hadn't healed completely. As she caught her breath and her breathing began to slow, he made his way back up the bed, shifting her so that she was no longer diagonal, and he had room to lie back with her in the crook of his arm.

They lay in silence for a while, each just happy to be with

the other, touching so intimately. Henry stroked her arm that was under his hand and Opal rubbed small circles on his chest.

Her head rested on his arm, her face against his chest, and he felt it when she smiled.

"That was even better than the girls said it was. Maybe their husbands don't know how to do it as well as you do."

A low laugh rumbled out of him. "Stroking my ego on that subject may have about the same result as stroking something else of mine. Besides, we haven't gotten to the main event yet. I could still turn out to be lousy at this."

Opal laughed and slapped his chest playfully. "Then you'd better bring your best efforts if you're going to top that. Don't forget—it's supposed to be your job to teach me all these things the way you like them. You wouldn't want me to be one of those women who just lies there and repeats the times tables in her head, would you?"

He burst out laughing. "I do believe your married friends have already advanced you beyond that point. I'm curious, though," he said. "Tell me what else they shared with you."

"Well, that was probably the biggest thing. I'm not sure I want to share anything else—I might lose my advantage."

"Advantage? This isn't a game, you know, sweetheart. We're on the same side here. The side where we both win big."

"I know, but surprising you was fun. I like to think I could still do that."

"All right, fair enough. Tell me, did your friends share anything you thought was odd? Or might be unpleasant?"

"Not that I want to talk about," she said as she laughed. "Wouldn't want to give you any ideas."

He chuckled again. "Oh, darlin'," he said, "I'm almost certain I've already had all those ideas. Believe me, men can dream up a lot of things that a naked man and a naked woman can do together."

"I daresay women can, too."

"You think so? Anything you dream up, I'm willing to give it a try."

He felt the smile spread across her face against his chest again.

———

WHEN OPAL AWOKE, she was closer to her side of the bed and Henry was still sleeping on his back. She was glad they were no longer entwined; she needed to relieve herself and she didn't want to wake him.

He'd left a lantern on in the bathroom for her benefit. She was able to take care of her needs and return to bed without interrupting his sleep. As she lay there thinking of the intimate things that had happened between them, she felt her own need rising again. She touched her breasts and nipples and let her hands drift down further. She found her little pearl and stroked it like Henry had earlier.

Opal wondered why she'd never stroked herself like this before. *It would be so simple to satisfy myself.* As she rubbed and explored her body, she realized her own desire made her wet again, nearly as wet as Henry had made her earlier. Scooting over a few inches, she took Henry's member in her hand and gently stroked it in undulating movements. He stirred but didn't wake. She kept on, unsure of her plan at this point.

He stirred more and may have murmured something in his sleep. She couldn't tell if it was dream-words or simply a subconscious groan.

As she increased the tempo of her hand movements, he spoke. "Opal? What are you trying to do?" he asked huskily, still hoarse from sleep.

"I believe I'm doing it and not just trying anymore. My new friend here has sprung up to say hello to me."

"He has definitely sprung up. Clearly, he likes it when you start conversations with him. Must be a fine friendship you've struck up."

"I'm becoming quite fond of him. Henry," she said, a little more seriously, "I want him inside me. I want to be your wife in that way, too. Please don't make me wait."

"You know what Elliott said."

"I do, but I also know how the injury felt when you loved me earlier. It didn't hurt, Henry, and I don't think it'll hurt me if you go ahead and make love to me now."

"There's a big difference, sweetie. My hand and mouth weren't that aggressive. A man's body, well, the act requires more forcefulness. I could hurt you, and I don't want to do that."

"Please, Henry, I want to be yours. I want to feel you inside me. Even if I don't find completion, I just want you to make me yours. You can stop after that, and I'll finish you with my mouth like I did earlier. Please."

"Oh, darlin'," he said as he closed the distance between them on the bed and kissed her. His hand wandered to her breast and his lips followed. The same hand wandered down between her legs and he was surprised that she was already primed for him. Henry nudged her legs apart and positioned himself on his knees between them. His left hand teased her pearl as his right one positioned his hardness at her opening, just touching it.

With a look at her first, he shoved inside and stilled himself to let her adjust.

"Are you all right, darlin'?"

"Yes," she said as she shifted her hips slightly. "I want all of you."

He groaned as he slowly slid his length inside her and stopped again.

"Oh, sweet Opal. You feel so good. So good," he whispered.

"Yes," she whispered back. "And I don't hurt, either from my injuries or from it being my first time."

He managed a short chuckle. "I haven't begun the energetic part yet, darlin'. Don't speak too soon."

He slowly withdrew and slowly pushed back in. He wanted her to learn the feel of him, and besides, he wanted to savor it, too. Henry continued at this pace until she begged him for more. He sped up some, still afraid of jarring her too much.

It wasn't long before her moans and mewls and whispers had him almost ready. He put his weight on his left arm and moved his right hand to her little cluster of nerve endings to bring about her release more quickly. As soon as she arched, he let himself sink into her again and spend.

Her breathing heavy, she smiled as she said, "Now I truly feel like your wife."

"Well, wife, wait here. I'll be right back."

He was wiping himself with one wet cloth as he walked back in carrying another wet cloth and a towel. "Let me clean you up some, sweetie."

"Please do. I'm used to that, you know. Once I'm all healed, I may have forgotten how to take care of myself."

EIGHT

Their Sunday was just as satisfying and intimate as their Saturday had been.

She couldn't talk him into more vigorous relations again, but they both found that their hands, mouths and tongues were more than enough. Henry even thought it was more emotionally satisfying that way. He was getting to know her in a way he hadn't with any other women before. It made him feel even closer to Opal.

Henry had cooked breakfast and made a light lunch. Opal finally convinced him she could help with supper preparation and he capitulated. He handed her a knife and a bowl with a few potatoes and an onion. "There. You cut. I'll fry."

"Yes, sir," she said, smiling up at him.

"Opal, do you know how to use a gun?"

"No. I've never even held one."

"We're going to remedy that. You need to know how to handle one."

"You really think I need to?"

"I do, especially if we get chickens like you mentioned. You aren't in a big city anymore. There are all kinds of varmints roaming around here. I've had to kill rattlesnakes in the yard." He paused, turned to her and softened his tone. "And you realize those killers know by now that a woman survived. If they tried very hard, they might be able to track you down."

She stopped peeling. "I know. I didn't really want to deal with it, though."

"I think we have to, sweetie. I'll stay with you every minute I can, but there will be times when I have to be away. I want to know you'll be able to take care of yourself."

"Maybe I could go visit with Amy or Nessa when you have to be away?"

"You can do that sometimes, but it's not a permanent solution. Ultimately, you need to know how to shoot."

She sighed. "You're right."

He took the fried ham out of the skillet and sat down with a knife to help her finish the potatoes and onion. "Good. We'll get a new gun for you tomorrow while we're getting supplies. I think you'll enjoy it, sweetie. It'll boost your confidence." He winked at her.

After supper, Opal insisted on washing dishes by herself. Henry acquiesced. While she washed, he set about preparing a hot bath for them to share.

He came up behind her, startling her, and she jumped when he began to unbutton her dress in the back.

"You frightened me!" She put her hands on the counter and chuckled.

He pulled the dress off her shoulders and let it drop to the floor.

"Henry! We're in the kitchen. It's not dark yet."

"The curtains are drawn, darlin'. Nobody can see in." He pulled the shift over her head then untied and removed her bloomers.

He turned her toward him and leaned down to kiss the scar

on her shoulder, trailing a path across her chest and down enough to kiss the scars on her side.

She lovingly put one hand on his shoulder, the other in his hair.

"There was a fleeting moment on that stagecoach when I was afraid you wouldn't want me anymore now that I'd have scars."

He stood and looked into her eyes then pulled her into a tight hug.

"I should take you over my knee for a thought like that. You've healed enough now for me to do it, you know. There's nothing that would make me not want you."

She pulled back and laughed a little, touching his face. "I know that now; I don't have any doubts about it. But I hadn't met you yet. And I'd lost a lot of blood. Clear thinking wasn't necessarily taking place, I don't think."

"Sweetie, you thought clearly enough to make your way home to me. I'm mighty glad you did. Come on," he said, pulling her away. "Our bath is ready."

———

THAT NIGHT when they were asleep, Opal was unusually restless and fitful. She made a few noises in her sleep and sounded frightened. Henry felt her pull away from him and move her hands in the air in front of her.

"No! No. No, don't," she said in a slow, labored dream-voice. Then she screamed.

"Opal. Wake up, darlin'," Henry cooed to her as he gently shook her and reached to put his arms around her.

She fought against him before he managed to get her awake enough to realize she'd had a nightmare. Henry could feel her fast heartbeat. She wept for a few minutes as he held her.

"I was on the stagecoach. It was happening again—all those people getting shot. All the blood."

He rocked her in his arms, soothing her as he might have comforted a baby. "It was a bad dream, sweetheart, just those bad memories coming out. Want me to get you a glass of water?"

"No, just hold me for a while."

"Let's lie back down and I'll hold you while you go back to sleep."

OPAL AWOKE none the worse for having had the nightmare. Henry had promised to show her the town and take her out to eat breakfast and to buy supplies and groceries, and she looked forward to it.

They were both in happy moods, holding hands as they walked into Mary's restaurant. When Mary saw them, she clasped her hands together and called out a welcome from halfway across the room. Mary was a short, stout, round woman, and she crossed the room in what looked like dangerously fast steps for such short legs.

"You must be our Opal!" she said and pulled Opal down just a bit while she tiptoed and planted a kiss on her cheek. "I can't tell you how happy I am to meet you. I want you to know I think your husband is one fine man, a good man. I hope you two are as happy as my husband and I are. His name's Henry, too. Maybe Henrys are just good men, don't you think?"

"They must be; I know mine's a good one." She put her hand on Mary's arm. "Mary, I want to thank you for the food you sent for us while I was recuperating at Amy's. That was awfully thoughtful of you."

"Well, of course, you're welcome, but there's no need for thanks. We take care of each other in this town. Always have, since I've lived here, anyway." Even as she said it, she was on her way back to the kitchen. "Have a seat somewhere. I'll bring you coffees and the breakfast special."

Opal looked at Henry and briefly widened her eyes as a silent comment about Mary's exuberance.

Henry chuckled. "She's excitable. Everybody loves Mary. Darn good cook, too. Just wait until you taste the food."

It wasn't long before Mary returned with two cups of coffee, a big grin on her round face. "Now would you prefer peach preserves or blackberry jam? Oh, never mind, I'll bring both." She said the last sentence as she made her way back to the kitchen.

Opal got that look again, and Henry chuckled but changed the subject.

"When we're through eating, I want to drive you around town and show you where everything is. I'd like to take you out to visit the sawmill and the big building where we make and sell furniture. Then, last, we can head to the mercantile and do some shopping. How does that sound?"

"It sounds like a perfect day. Oh, I'd like to wire Ben and let him know we're married now, and he can ship my books and the rest of my things."

"We can do that."

Just then, Arthur and Harriet Smithers came in and sat down. Once seated, Harriet saw Opal and excitedly jumped up to go to their table. She took the younger woman's hand in hers. "Opal, it's so good to see you up and about. It looks like Henry's been taking good care of you."

"Yes, he has."

"Hello, Harriet," Henry said. By then, Arthur had joined his wife. "Arthur, good to see you too," he said as he held out his hand for a handshake.

"Mrs. Tucker, we haven't met yet. I'm Harriet's husband,

Arthur. I can't tell you how happy we are to see you up and around and happily married. It does my heart good."

"Thank you, Mr. Smithers."

"Oh no, dear, please call me Arthur."

"Thank you, Arthur, and I'm Opal," she said, smiling up at him.

"Now, you two," Harriet began, "one evening soon, Arthur and I would like to drop in and give you a little welcome gift. It's really nothing much, just something we feel every married couple should have. I promise we won't stay very long. We wouldn't want to monopolize a young couple still on their honeymoon."

"Would you like to come for dinner, say, this evening?" Opal asked.

"No, dear, we won't impose in that way; you're still newly-weds. Tell you what, we'll come this evening after dinnertime, and I'll even bring a dessert for us all to enjoy. I promise we won't stay more than a few minutes."

Henry spoke for them. "We look forward to seeing you then."

OPAL ENJOYED the tour of the sawmill and workshop where they made the furniture. She was amazed at the fine pieces they produced; she had expected the final products to be more rustic in keeping with her idea of the untamed west. Instead, most of the pieces showed fine craftsmanship and artistry. It pleased Henry when she said the furniture was even nicer than some she'd seen in fine, expensive homes she'd visited back in Omaha. She picked out a few pieces on the spot that she wanted for the house.

Henry slowly drove their wagon through the town, showing

her the businesses and the homes of friends of theirs who lived in town. Some folks were out on the sidewalks and he stopped a few times to introduce them to his wife. Everyone knew her story and without fail, they told her they'd prayed for her and were happy to see how healthy she looked. She was touched by their kindness.

At the mercantile, Henry asked to see Clint's handgun selection. He had Opal pick them all up to see how they felt in her hand and see how easy it was for her to use the barrel sights. She narrowed it down to two models but couldn't decide, so Henry told Clint he'd take them both. One was a Colt Navy and the other was a Remington Double Derringer. Opal thought the Derringer was cute.

That afternoon, Henry wanted to get started on Opal's shooting lessons. He painted a small circle on a piece of wood and filled it in with paint, then he put a larger concentric circle around it. He nailed the target to a pointed stake and put it in a spot toward the back of their property, where no stray shots would endanger anyone.

"All right, darlin', this is how you hold it, with your right hand. Then you put your left underneath to help steady it. See? Two things to remember. One, is that you squeeze the trigger. If you try to pull it toward you, you'll lose your aim. The other thing is recoil. It'll push back at you. And, it's noisy."

"Got it. May I try?"

"Sure, here. That's it. Before you squeeze, be sure to look down the barrel and line up the sights. Fire when you're ready, and don't forget the recoil."

Opal took a deep breath and squeezed. They immediately heard the sound of the wooden target being hit.

"I hit it!"

"You sure did, darlin'," Henry said, even more proud than she was. "Let's go look."

Her shot was outside the center circle but within the outer one. "That's excellent, sweetie. Look how close to the center you got."

"I want to do it again!" Her excitement was contagious.

She shot a few more times, each time staying in the radius of the outer circle but not quite hitting center. Henry let her shoot for quite a while so he could show her how to reload the guns, too. He loved to see that she enjoyed it and took to it so well.

After about an hour and a half of target practice, Henry said it was enough for one day and she should fire the bullets that were in the guns, then they'd go in and he'd show her how to clean them.

She emptied the Derringer then picked up the Colt revolver. She made respectable shots on the first five, even getting right on the rim of the inner circle. Opal sighted the last shot, then pulled it back and looked at Henry.

"Let's make this fun. If I hit the center circle with this last shot, then we have full-fledged, grown-up, energetic sex tonight. Regardless of what Elliott says. Deal?" She eyed him with one brow raised and a smirk on her face.

Henry didn't think she'd do it since she hadn't in nearly two hours.

"I'll take that bet." He grinned.

Opal turned back to the target, raised her arms, steadied, sighted, and squeezed.

Bullseye.

Henry laughed. "I believe you've been holding back. That might get you in trouble, girlie. Almost like lying to me, you know? If you're up for that kind of sex, you're up for a hidin'."

Opal laughed and ran back to the house, with him not far behind ,carrying the guns and the ammunition.

AFTER AN EARLY SUPPER, they cleared off the table and Henry straightened up and swept the public areas of the house while Opal tidied the kitchen. She put on a fresh pot of coffee and a pot of water for tea, just in case. They wanted to be ready for when the Smitherses arrived.

They didn't have to wait long at all.

"Come on in," Henry welcomed them, motioning with his hand to enter.

"I brought a peach cobbler. I hope you both like it," Harriet said.

"I never met a cobbler I didn't like," Henry said.

Opal laughed a little. "It's true—he has a sweet tooth. Would you like coffee or tea to go with it?"

Henry motioned for them to sit at the kitchen table. He got bowls for the cobbler.

Arthur carried a pretty wooden box but didn't mention it. Neither did Henry nor Opal.

"I'd like tea if you have it, dear," Harriet said.

"I will in about three minutes," she said as she poured the hot water over the loose tea in the teapot.

Henry set a small pitcher of cream on the table.

When they were all settled with drinks and dessert, Harriet got around to the purpose of their visit. "Arthur and I have been very happily married for all these years, and we like to share our secret with newlyweds who may not have quite found their way yet. It hurts me to see marriages that are unhappy. I want everyone to be as happy and as much in love as Arthur and I are."

"That's a lovely thought," Opal said. She put her hand on Henry's arm. "I think we're off to a fine start."

"Oh, we are so pleased to hear it, Opal. I do hope your relationship only strengthens from here on. Mail order marriages are so different, you know, and I would feel terrible if I had any part of making a poor match," Harriet replied.

Arthur inserted himself into the conversation. He looked at Opal as he spoke. "You must realize your relationship is vastly different from most marriages. Not only were you a mail order union, but the most unfortunate circumstances befell you on your way here. You're only now getting back to your old robust health. You're just now beginning to experience what most would consider the normalcy of a married relationship."

"Yes, I suppose that is true," Opal said, remembering that they were only now going to have "robust" relations and only because she had won a bet.

"This is an intensely private topic, but we want to share our thoughts and give you a little item you might use if you wish. If nothing else, please keep it around as a reminder. Arthur, please let them open it now."

Arthur put the wooden box on the table and scooted it toward the younger couple.

"Go ahead and open it, sweetie," Henry said.

"Angus and Nessa said you might give us a little gift. They didn't say what it was, though," Opal said.

Arthur grinned. "No, I suppose not."

Opal opened the box and began unwrapping several layers of pretty paper. When she saw the paddle, she almost dropped it. She looked up in surprise.

Henry took it from her and laughed, turning it over in his hand. He ran his fingers over the ornate, carved, reversed letters, realizing that when it was applied to a backside, the cursive word *Obey* would appear on the skin. "Well, that big Irish scalawag. I'd recognize Angus' work anywhere. He didn't say a word to me about these. You see, Opal? It's the same script as your name on your new bookcase." He laughed again. "Only, it isn't reversed on the furniture."

Harriet smiled. "Yes, we asked Angus to make them for all the mail order unions. He'll be happy to put Opal's name on the other side if you like. That's what he did on Nessa's and Tillie Snow's and mine," she added.

"You mean, you all have..." Opal asked, her eyes wide again.

"Yes, dear, we do. Now I realize Deacon and Tillie weren't one of our mail order unions, but given what Angus knew of their relationship, he made one for them. And we asked him to make one for us."

Opal and Henry looked at each other, not quite knowing what to think of this insight into other couples' marriages.

"Now here's the decision you must make, whether to use it for its intended purpose or not," Arthur said. "I'll get right to the point. Opal. I have no idea about your conduct or your temperament. They may be exemplary, and if they are, then good for you. But, Henry, in the event you find that she disobeys or flies off the handle or doesn't act as you expect her to, I urge you to use it. Of course, if you're like me, you won't always use a paddle. Belts and crops are effective on Harriet. Straps, yardsticks, hairbrushes and bath brushes, too. You get the idea."

Neither Henry nor Opal knew quite how to respond, but neither of them missed the doting and adoring look Harriet gave her husband.

"And I would add that even if your conduct and temperament are exemplary, there might be a need for reminders. It helps to be reminded of our proper roles now and then. Sometimes that little paddle and those other items Arthur mentioned can, well, keep the ardor in a relationship from getting stale. This is how we've kept our marriage fresh for nearly twenty five years now," Harriet said.

"Well, you've certainly given us something to think about," Henry replied.

Harriet laughed. "You're going to have to do more than think about it! I urge you to try it out, and the sooner the better. I assure you, Arthur doesn't hesitate to tear into me good when it's warranted. Why, I don't know if you've heard the story yet, but when we were new in town and still living in the hotel, Arthur got so put out with my cranky behavior that he made me carry around a big wooden spoon so it would always be handy, no matter where we were. I got well acquainted with the kitchen in Mary's restaurant." Harriet laughed at the memories.

Opal was a little shocked, but she hid it.

"Harriet, dear," Arthur said, "we've kept this young couple long enough. We should leave them to their privacy." He stood to take Harriet's arm and help her up.

"I'm going to leave you the rest of the cobbler. There's enough left so you can enjoy a midnight snack and dessert tomorrow. I can get my dish sometime later. There's no rush."

"Well, thank you for the cobbler," Opal said. "It's delicious."

Harriet laughed again. "I noticed you didn't thank us for the paddle, dear. That's all right." She pulled Opal into a hug, and Opal realized it was because she wanted to whisper something to her.

"Opal," the older woman whispered, "let him warm up your backside real good. You wouldn't believe how much more passionate the sex can be."

Opal tried not to register the shock on her facial expression, but she failed.

"We should get together for tea one morning, dear. I get together often with Amy and Evie Glover, the deputy's wife. We always enjoy ourselves. You should join us."

"Yes, I'd like that," Opal said.

HENRY CLOSED the door behind the Smitherses after their goodbyes. Opal walked back to the table and picked up the dirty bowls and cups and put them in the sink to wash. Henry put the lid back on the cobbler dish, set it on the counter, and wiped off the table.

He picked up the paddle and admired the workmanship again.

"So, do you think we should put this to use?" he asked, a smirk on his face.

"As kindling?"

He laughed. "No, I don't think so. That Angus. This really is fine work. And for a paddle!"

"I'm a little uncomfortable that you like it so much," she said, not appearing uncomfortable at all.

"I'm thinking I might use it. You did fool me today with the target practice. It's not nice to fool your husband, you know."

She heard the teasing in his voice and wasn't worried. "I wasn't fooling you. I just got lucky with that last shot. I'd been trying to do that the whole time." She grinned mischievously at him over her shoulder as she continued washing the dishes.

"Um hmm," he said.

"It's true!"

He came up behind her quietly and quickly, and before she knew he was there, he gave her bottom a quick swat.

"Yeow!" she said, dropping a cup back into the water.

"I know that didn't hurt. Too many layers and I didn't swing very hard."

"No, but it startled me," she said with a chuckle.

"Got to admit, it was kind of fun."

"Henry!"

"I may end up using this little item."

"Again, I say, for kindling? Firewood?"

"No, ma'am, I don't think so. I want to see *Obey* appear on your backside. I think I'll have Angus put your name on the other side. I mean, we can't let Nessa's paddle be nicer than yours."

"*Henry!*"

"Aw, come on, darlin'," he said, "it might be fun. Hey, what did Harriet say when she hugged you? Looked like she was whispering something, and I saw the look on your face."

"Oh, it was nothing really."

Henry let another lick hit her bottom, again, not hard. "Try that again, sweetie."

"Really, it wasn't anything special."

He swatted again. "Opal, darlin', I can do this all night," he said with a laugh.

"Oh, all right." She turned to face him. "She said I should let you warm my bottom because the sex will be more intense afterward."

Henry burst out laughing. "Well, that's blunt. No wonder you had that look on your face. She may not be wrong, though."

"What? You... you... have experienced this before?" She looked at him with questioning disbelief.

Henry looked at her, considering whether or not he should tell her. But she asked, so he decided honesty would be best. "I told you in my letter that, unlike yours, my own past isn't pure."

"I would expect that of a man your age."

"I've never been in love before you, I want you to know that. But there was a woman back where I came from. She worked in a brothel and liked to have men spank her. And there were men who liked to spank, so she had a steady stream of clients."

"And you were one of them?"

"It wasn't always her I visited, but once in a while, yes."

"Let's go sit down. I want to hear all about this." She eyed him with a salacious gleam and dried her hands on her apron.

"Are you telling me you want to hear about me with another woman? I'd be spitting nails if our roles were reversed here."

"Well, we're safe. I have no experience for you to worry about. The closest thing I've come to it is hearing other married ladies talk about their husbands. Now, tell me. Tell me everything. You told me you'd keep yourself only to me from now on, and I believe you. I'm not naïve enough to believe you lived under a rock until I came along." She laughed at the expression on his face. "Now I might learn how you got so good at that thing you do with your tongue."

Henry eyed her and grinned. They settled into the couch, his arm around her.

"I'm all ears now. Spill those beans."

He didn't know where to start, and he said so.

"Tell me about a typical visit to this woman. Your first visit. We can go from there."

"All right. In this particular place, the ladies always offered to bathe you first. That's not common in a lot of brothels. It was kind of a high class place. Some mine workers used to come in on a weekend, filthy, so I can understand the bath part. The women get naked to do it, too, so there's that. The first time I went, I didn't know about this lady's proclivities. She got me clean, and of course, got me all hot and hard in the process. Then she said, 'Did you know that spankings sting more on wet skin?' I said I didn't know."

Henry shifted a bit in his seat and Opal noticed his growing length. Knowing that he was getting aroused affected her, too.

He continued. "She said it definitely does. She said, 'I love it when a man takes control and spanks my wet bottom.' She asked me if I'd do that for her. It occurred to me that since I was paying for this session, she should be catering to my desires, but it hit me real quick that this might end up being one of my desires, and I just didn't realize it yet. I'd had whippins all my life and never thought they were remotely sexual. But my best friend had a sister and I was there a time or two when she got one. I thought there was something wrong with me for getting aroused by it. I was about to learn there was nothing wrong with it at all."

Opal put her hand on his crotch, urging him to continue his story.

"So we got out of the tub and she bent over it, sticking her butt out. 'Give me a good hard slap on my ass,' she said. So I did. She yelped and asked for another one, then another. Next, she wanted to lie across my lap while I sat on a chair. 'Give it to me good,' she said. 'I've been a bad, bad girl.' So I let loose with a few good ones. She kept screaming out 'yes' and things a person receiving a real spanking would say, like, 'I won't do it again' and 'I'm sorry'. I guess I got into the spirit of things, because I started saying things like, 'I hope you learn your lesson' and 'you're going to be even sorrier.' Her ass was turning bright red and I loved how it looked, knowing I'd made it red. At one point, I started swatting halfway to her knees, and I didn't let up. Her legs trembled and kicked. I was worried that I was taking it too far until she spread her legs and I could see what it was doing to her."

"She was wet?" Opal asked.

"Sopping, dripping down on my legs. 'Touch me,' she said. And, well, you know me, I did."

Opal giggled.

"It didn't take much touching before she had her release. I just stroked her a little. I was amazed. After that, she dragged me to the bed and pounced on me. She kept telling me to slap her ass, and she had me in positions I'd never tried before."

Opal looked at him skeptically.

"What? I was a young kid. Probably about eighteen or nineteen. That woman taught me almost everything I know," he said, laughing. He reached for Opal's breast. "Turned out, she liked having her breasts slapped, too, but not quite as hard. She really liked having her nipples pinched hard and flicked hard with a fingernail. I tried that on my own nipples, and it hurt like hell, but she craved it."

Opal pulled her skirt up and put his hand at her crotch. He was surprised to find it bare, with no bloomers. "Maybe I just learned some things, too. Henry, I want to try... more things. Is that all right?"

"Darlin', are you sure?"

"More than you can know. Some of those ladies I talked to mentioned things like this, but I couldn't imagine. Now, the way you explained it, I think I might get it."

Henry pulled her up and then bent her over the couch. After he pulled up her skirts, he asked her again, "Are you sure?"

"Yes, but please start easy."

He gave her bottom a few swats, not too hard but definitely enough to sting. He rubbed. He swatted her again, and she began to moan. "Does that hurt?"

"Not really. It stings some, though."

"More?"

She was embarrassed at her answer. "Yes."

Henry swatted a little harder a few times then rubbed. The rubbing wasn't gentle anymore. She was dripping wet. "Oh, darlin', I don't think I'm going to last much longer. I'm about to explode."

"Then do it now," she practically screamed, "hard!"

THE FELL asleep in each other's arms about an hour later, exhausted from their 'full-fledged, grown-up, energetic sex.' Sometime later in the night, Opal began to whimper and jerk, and it woke Henry. He put his free arm around her, but she fought him off.

"No! Stop," she cried, and he realized by the halted, struggling sound of her voice that she was still asleep.

He gently shook her. "Wake up, sweetie."

"Get away!" Her hands clawed at the air in front of her, warding away something unseen.

"Opal," he said more firmly and loudly, shaking her again.

This time she roused, disoriented. She panicked for a moment before she realized she'd been dreaming, then she started crying softly.

"It was that nightmare again, wasn't it?" Henry asked, stroking her hair.

She nodded. "Almost the same. I was in the coach and they were about to shoot. Jed—I saw Jed's hand." Opal sat up abruptly. "Henry, I remember something about the one named Jed. He had a red birthmark on his right hand, his gun hand. It was a port wine stain that covered nearly half the back of his hand and onto his thumb."

"Are you sure, sweetheart? That could help them identify the man. Are you sure it wasn't just in the dream?"

"No. I remember seeing his hand in the stage. I never got a good look at his face because the coach wall blocked it most of the time, but he stuck his hand in the doorway. I got a clear look at it. It may have been a burn, but I'm almost positive it was a skin discoloration."

"We'll let Jim know tomorrow. That's a useful piece of information. Let's get some sleep now." He wiped her tears and she settled back into his arms.

THE NEXT MORNING, they spoke of the dream again.

"Do you remember any other new details about the men?"

"No," she said, pouring their coffee. "Just the birthmark."

"What about his height? Did he seem tall or short?"

She thought. "I don't have a sense of that, being up in the coach like I was."

"Was there anything odd about his speech? High or low voice?"

"Not high or low, but there was an uneducated quality; it's hard to describe. I remember the ringleader—Malachi—had a deep, raspy voice with an English accent. It was distinct."

"Why don't we go after breakfast and talk to Jim?" Henry asked. It was a question, but it meant they would go.

As Opal was cleaning up after breakfast, Henry took a cup of coffee to his spot on the couch, nearest the fire. Something caught his eye and he chuckled under his breath. There was a short wooden box on the hearth, only about nine inches tall and maybe fourteen or sixteen inches long. It was where they kept the kindling. Sitting amid the small sticks and twigs was the paddle. While she wasn't watching, he moved it to the dresser in the bedroom, wondering how long it would take her to notice.

"Henry, can we drop off the laundry with Mrs. Bracken on our way to the sheriff's office?" Opal asked as she hung her apron on its designated hook.

"Of course, we can. I was planning to take the buggy anyway, so we'll have room. It's threatening to rain."

"Perfect," she said, smiling. "How about I go bundle them up while you get the horses ready?"

"I'll do that very thing," he said as he kissed her cheek and headed out to the barn.

The laundry bundle was a huge drawstring bag made out of a thick cotton duck fabric, very heavy when full of dirty clothes and linens. Opal filled it and left it for Henry to tote.

Henry brought the buggy up in front of the house and went

inside for the bag and to get his wife. As he swung the heavy bag over his shoulder, he noticed the paddle was already back in the kindling box. He grinned and made a mental note to move it again when they got home.

———

HENRY *HYAHED* the horses while gently whipping the reins.

"Opal, it's probably time I went back to work, at least part time. Angus has been doing some of my workload, too, and I hate to ask him to do that any more than I have to."

"We knew you'd have to sometime," she said, a rueful smile on her face. "As much as I wish you could stay with me all day, I know you have to work."

He took her hand. "The question is whether or not you want to stay home alone or stay with Amy for the day tomorrow. We can take each day as it comes and decide until you think you're ready to stay on your own. If you want to stay with Amy, I'd like to let Jim know when we get there."

"I'm ready now. I'm a big girl and I can hit a bullseye. I'll be just fine by myself. You go on back to work and don't worry about me." She squared her shoulders as if to show him her resolve and determination.

"Well, all right, then," Henry said as he grinned and squeezed her hand, stopping the team in front of the sheriff's office.

"Hi, Jim," Opal said as they walked into the jailhouse.

Jim brightened. "Well, there's our girl. I sure am glad to see you doing so well," he said as he took his feet off his desk to stand and greet her with a hug.

"Thank you. Yes, I think I'm about healed now. And thanks again for all you and Amy did for me."

"We were happy to help. I hope you know that."

"I do, but still, I'm grateful."

Henry spoke up. "Has there been progress in finding the killers?"

"Some, but not much. Malachi Stone is said to have a hideout somewhere north of Separation. Reed and Deacon are up there trying to find him. They're with deputies from Rawlins. Nobody seems to know anything about Jed or the other man."

"Last night, Opal remembered something about Jed that may help identify him. Opal?"

"Well," she said, holding up her right hand and drawing an imaginary line, "his gun hand has a big port wine stain birthmark on the back of it. It goes from just this side of his pinkie and cuts across and covers the first knuckle of his thumb. It covers more than half the back of his hand."

"She said it could possibly be a burn mark, but she didn't think it was because the skin was smooth and not scarred," Henry added.

"That could definitely be helpful. I've seen criminals apprehended solely on identifiers like that. I'll get that out on the wire today."

"SO, DARLIN'," Henry said as they neared home, "what do you think we should do this afternoon? It'll be the last weekday afternoon we'll have together for a while, you know."

Opal looked all around then took Henry's hand in one of hers. With the other one, she pulled up her dress enough to put his hand between her legs.

"You little vixen, you," he said, giving her a sexy grin. "Not wearing bloomers! Tell me what's on your mind."

"I know what we should do this afternoon. We can start

once you pull the buggy in the barn. You could undo your britches and I could straddle you right here on the seat."

"What if we scare the horses?" he said, laughing.

"There are hay bales out there; we could use those."

"Sounds like a good start."

"Then afterward, we can go in the house. I think a bath would be nice. Maybe we can think of something to do in the bath."

"I like how you think."

Henry pulled the buggy into the barn and helped her down. He unhooked the horses and glanced over at Opal. She struggled but managed to move one hay bale next to a stack of two. As he finished taking care of the animals, he occasionally glanced in her direction to see what she was doing. She went to the back of the barn and picked up some horse blankets then walked back to the bales and covered them, two blanket layers deep. The next time he looked up, she'd unbuttoned her shirt and already had it off and was working on taking off her skirt and petticoat. He leaned against the stall wall, arms crossed across his chest, wondering how he could make this even more fun and interesting.

She turned toward him and gave him her sultriest look, lifting her hand and crooking her finger to beckon him.

"Not yet, darlin'. Take off your shift."

"I want to leave it on out here; we can work around it."

His slow smirk unnerved her a little. "I said, take off your shift."

"Henry, I—"

"Take it off."

She continued to look at him and didn't immediately do as he said. He slowly lifted one arm and took down the riding crop that hung on a nail in front of him.

"I'm waiting, and I'm becoming less patient." The smile on his face contrasted with his words.

She reached down to the hem and pulled the shift up and over her head, tossing it onto the pile of her clothes.

"That's better, but it's going to cost you. Now step up on that lower bale and sit on the higher one. That's it. Now spread your legs. All the way."

She slowly obeyed, and it was clear to him this wasn't what she had planned. It amused him.

"Touch yourself like you were doing when I walked in on you."

Her hands went to her breasts, rubbing and squeezing them until her nipples were hard.

"Now take one hand down lower. Dip your fingers inside, now in and out, like that. Faster. Look how wet you are, darlin', I can see it from here."

Henry unbuttoned his britches and drawers and reached in to stroke himself.

"Now take out your fingers—look how wet they are. Put 'em in your mouth and suck. Mmm, yes. Put 'em back inside you, then rub that little sweet spot. Use your other hand inside you, three fingers this time. That's it, keep doing that. Keep your legs spread so I can see."

His own motions sped up.

He took a deep breath. "Darlin', I love watching you do this. But when I can't take it any longer, I'm going to come over there and fuck you so hard and so fast, you'll think you've seen Heaven. People over in Laramie County are going to hear you scream."

Opal caught her breath and quickened her pace. Henry loved watching her; it was clear she was becoming highly aroused.

He slowly walked toward her. "Are you getting yourself

ready for me?"

"Yes."

"I think while I'm holding this crop, you should call me 'sir'. Let's do this again. Are you getting yourself ready for me?"

"Yes, sir."

"Stop touching yourself."

She did. He took her hand and sensuously licked the fingers that had been inside her. Then he stood back and touched the end of the crop to her nipples; he first teased one, then the other. He flicked them gently, but she was tense and flinched each time. She put her hands up and covered her breasts.

"No, no, darlin', none of that. Put your hands down."

He flicked again, concentrating on her hard right tip. Henry watched her fists clench as he quickened the pace and intensity of the flicks. He was gentle, but he knew a throb was building.

Opal protested with a whimper. He transferred the crop to his left hand and comforted her pinkened breast with his right.

"I think you might have liked that. Let's see what else you can take. Up on your knees on the lower bale and rest your chest and head on the tall one. Rest your head on your arms. That's good. Now spread. Make plenty of room for me."

She got into position. Henry's hand caressed her thighs and buttocks, dipping down between her legs to her wetness. He rubbed his hand over her sex, not letting it linger anywhere.

"One more thing before I fuck you. I want to remind you not to hesitate when I tell you to do something. Understand?"

"Yes."

Crack! Her cry of surprise followed.

"What did you say?"

"I meant yes, sir."

"That's much better. When we're in a situation such as this, I heartily recommend you remember the new rules. They're very simple, only two of them. Call me *sir* at times like this, and obey me. Easy. Understand?"

"Yes, sir, I understand."

"Good girl. Because this is what happens if you forget." He swung and cracked the crop on her backside again, much harder than the first one.

She cried out and lifted her head and arms.

"Stay down, sweet. Don't get up. You mustn't get up."

Henry wondered how far he could take her in this scenario and decided he shouldn't push her further, at least not this time. She was doing much better than he expected thus far. He'd been hesitant to try this game with her because of what she'd endured. He was afraid her mind would associate lack of control with her experiences within the stagecoach. He hoped she would see it as a purely sexual scenario instead. So far it seemed to work as he'd hoped.

He took the crop and rubbed it lightly between her legs. He tapped her little cluster of nerves gently. It was swollen and highly sensitive, and it made her wiggle her hips.

Henry gave a low chuckle. "Nice to know the crop can deliver desirable feelings, too, isn't it?"

She still breathed heavily, her demeanor wary. But she turned her head and managed to give him a crooked grin. He felt immense relief.

"Yes, sir," she said as she stuck out her bottom again and wagged it back and forth.

Henry grinned and gave her light taps all around and finished with a few light, teasing swats on her backside. He made sure nothing delivered more than a slight sting.

He suddenly threw the crop to the ground. "Oh, darlin', I want you now." The height and angle were perfect for him and he entered her completely with one powerful thrust. Lust took control and he slammed into her, over and over, lost in the moment with no conscious thought. Intense sensations brought guttural sounds from him, but he had no idea he was making any sounds. His eyes were open, but he didn't see—he could only feel, so much so that he felt attuned to Opal's body, too. He felt the small contractions across her lower belly and groin that signaled she neared her climax. Henry thundered at his release and when she shuddered hers, he dropped to the lower bale, turning and bringing Opal onto his lap.

The sated smile on her face spoke volumes, and a grateful Henry held her hard.

Later, inside, while Opal poured scented oils in the tub, Henry moved the paddle to a corner of the kitchen countertop.

THE NEXT MORNING, Henry went to work after a quick breakfast and a powerful kiss. It had been a long time since he'd been at the mill and he wanted to be early.

Opal took her time cleaning up the kitchen and deciding what she'd fix for their meals that day. Henry said he'd be home for lunch, and she wanted to make something nice for him. She finally decided to go ahead and have a cold meal of meat, cheeses, bread, and pickles, but she made a custard pie for dessert because it was one of Henry's favorites.

She had a few minutes to spare so she pulled out the book she'd purchased for her train trip but never finished. Then she remembered, jumped up, ran to the kitchen, and grabbed the paddle so she could put it back in the kindling box. She inwardly smiled at their new little game.

Henry came home for lunch on time as promised, and they enjoyed their meal.

He said Jim had come to the mill to let him know that because of Opal's additional information, they had a strong lead on the man with the birthmark and the other one. "The name Jed wasn't familiar to the lawmen, but a couple of them remembered a red birthmark on the hand of a robber by the name of Jeremiah. They checked their records and found his last name is Helper. And sure enough, they found he has a brother named Herman Helper who seems to be his partner in crime. Thanks to you, sweetie, they now know who to look for. They're getting the information to Reed and Deacon today, too."

"I'm glad I'm able to help." She added ruefully, "Maybe I need to have more bad dreams."

After lunch, Opal tried to interest her husband in some afternoon relations, but he reluctantly pulled away. "You don't know how much I'd like to stay longer, but I need to get back to the mill. I promise, I'll make it up to you tonight. Full-fledged, grown-up, and very energetic sex. Acrobatic, even." He pulled her in for one more passionate kiss then left for work.

Opal cleaned up the lunch mess and set the rest of the pie aside for supper. She used some of the hot water to make a fresh pot of tea and poured a nice cup for herself before sitting down again with her book. She read and sipped for a couple of hours but needed to stand and stretch after sitting for so long. When she did, she noticed the paddle was no longer in the kindling box. When did he have time to move it? She walked through the house, haphazardly looking here and there to see if she could readily find it. She didn't. She decided to look in the bedroom next.

It wasn't on top of the dresser or his chest of drawers. It wasn't on either of the nightstands. She opened the wardrobe and ran her hand across his shirts. The scent of him reached her nostrils and she bunched up some of the shirts and brought them to her face. She inhaled his masculine, earthy, woody and woodsy scent that she loved. She thought of how she loved to smell that scent when they lay entwined in bed, and she had a visceral reaction to the olfactory memory. That led to thoughts of his touch upon her skin, and she dropped the shirts and reached up to touch her own breasts. She moaned, imagining Henry's hands on her.

Opal unbuttoned and shucked her shirt so she could feel herself better. She sensed her own wetness below as she tweaked and pinched her nipples. She hurriedly unbuttoned her skirt and let it drop, along with her petticoat. She wore no bloomers again today, so that left her only in her shift. She lay down on top of the bedcovers.

HENRY FINISHED WORK EARLY, eager to be able to hurry home and surprise Opal. Rains had left the streets muddy, so he removed his boots on the porch before coming inside. Besides, it would be easier to sneak up and surprise Opal in his stocking feet.

He expected to find her in the kitchen or parlor and was momentarily taken aback until he heard a sound coming from the back of the house. He crept down the hall to their bedroom, avoiding the wooden floorboard that he knew creaked. A look of amused pleasure came over his face when he began to recognize the sounds coming from their bedroom.

He silently made his way to the doorway of his own room. Opal was on the bed in only her bunched-up shift, her eyes closed, one hand on her breast and the other on her little pearl. Her two middle fingers were playing it like a fine instrument.

"Mmm," she moaned. "Yes, Henry, yes." Her fingers briefly dipped inside her wetness then went back to her nub.

Henry's hands silently unfastened his britches. He reached in and freed his hardness, stroking it as he watched Opal's fingers work on herself.

Her eyes still closed, she continued. "Henry, yes, like that." The pace of her fingers quickened, and her other hand flicked her nipple roughly, repeatedly, through the fabric of her shift. Her hips began to move. "Yes, Henry, yes. Oh! Henry, just a little more."

He silently made his way to the end of the bed. "May I join you, darlin'?"

Her eyes opened in an embarrassed panic and she shuffled awkwardly and jumped up. "Oh! I'm so sorry! I'm sorry. I won't do that again."

He quickly made his way to her and pushed her back down on the bed. "Why the hell not?" he asked.

"You... you aren't angry?"

"Angry? Hell no! I come home to find my wife giving herself pleasure with my name on her lips? Thinking about me while she's touching herself? No man alive would be angry at that. He's not much of a man if he is. It's hot as hell—knowing you think about me like that. Now get that shift off and help me out of my clothes. I'm about to make both our fantasies come true."

"TELL me again why you thought I'd be angry with you for that," Henry said much later as they were lying together in the aftermath.

"Some people think it's a sin, you know."

He laughed. "Well, not in this house, or I'd have been a condemned man long ago. I know people who say they agree with that, but I don't believe for a minute they actually do believe it, much less live it. Trust me on this one, darlin'. Men do it. I imagine a lot of women do, too." He hugged her to him for emphasis. "I'm glad you do, especially if you think about me while you're doing it. And *really* especially when it leads to what we just did. Hell, I think you should do it every day."

She playfully slapped his chest.

"Although, I think the next time I walk in on you like that, I'm not going to interrupt. I'll watch until you're finished."

"Then I'll want to watch you."

He grinned. "I have no problem with that. Then we can get together afterward."

Opal sighed and sat up on the side of the bed. "I better get up and put on the cornbread for supper."

He pulled her back down roughly and hovered over her. "A cold supper is fine. Right now I have other things on my mind."

His lips took hers roughly. The hand that wasn't bearing his weight went to her breast and squeezed and pinched her nipple, then he rubbed his fingernail back and forth over it, flicking it.

"They're still sensitive, be careful."

"I like it when they're so sensitive. Then when I do this, it makes you more edgy and needy. I love how it makes you squirm under me."

His lips moved down to her other breast and licked all around before drawing in a mouthful and giving it a hard, strong, unrelenting suck. She cried out, her hands grasping at the sheets. "Oh, Henry! I felt that all the way... down there."

"Down here?" he asked, thrusting two fingers inside her as his thumb found her pearl.

"Yes," she whispered.

"Or here?" he asked as he pulled his fingers from her sheath and quickly inserted one in her crinkled rosette before her body had a chance to protest.

"Oh! I'm not sure about—"

He cut her off, "Then get sure, darlin'. Because I like it. I want you to learn to like it, too."

They did have a cold supper, much later that night.

NINE

The days passed and Opal continued to regain her strength. Her wounds healed and Elliott pronounced her fit. They didn't share with him that they'd been acting as though she'd healed for weeks already.

It took her two days to find the paddle where he'd placed it —it was partly hidden under a stack of towels in the bathroom. But she found it and placed it back in the kindling box where Henry let it stay another day or two before moving it again. Whenever he left the house, the first thing Opal did was search high and low for the paddle so she could put it back. They never spoke of it.

The search for Malachi Stone and the Helper brothers hadn't yet been fruitful. Leads came in of possible sightings but didn't pan out; the outlaws were either misidentified or had left the area without leaving clues.

Reed and Deacon Snow had been on the road, searching for them, but had returned home to Big Rock to regroup and confer with the sheriff and deputy. The Rawlins police had been unable to glean any more information after learning that the family name of Jed and Herman was Helper. No one had been able to find any of their relatives or even confirm that they had any.

Henry felt bad that he hadn't been able to give Opal a proper honeymoon. One evening after supper, as they sat by the fire, he brought it up. "Darlin', since you're all better, what do you think about having that honeymoon I promised you? Things are going well at the sawmill and Angus said it wouldn't be a problem if we took off for a couple of weeks. We could go to Rawlins if you want. Hell, we can go anywhere you want, even across the country. I'll give you whatever you want, take you wherever you want."

"Oh, Henry, I swore on that train trip I wouldn't travel anymore unless it was back to Omaha to see Ben and Zora. But I don't think I want to go that far, at least for a while. Maybe in a few months but not yet."

"Well, how about just going up to Rawlins then? You know it's just under two days to get there—we only have to spend one night on the road. They've got two playhouses in town. We could see a couple of plays. Sometimes that big music house has traveling acts. We might hit it at the right time to see some performers there, too. And I found out they have a big store and one whole wall of it is books."

"Oh! A bookstore almost like one back home," Opal said. "And I do love to go to plays. All right, yes. That would be wonderful, Henry."

"All right then," Henry said as he broke out in a huge happy grin. "I'll let Angus know and we can get it scheduled. Let's go in the next week or two; what do you think?"

Opal knew the time of her monthly courses was coming up in a day or two. "How about week after next? That would be perfect."

"Consider it done, darlin'. Don't pack too much. I want to buy you some new things there."

"Henry!" Opal burst out as she jumped up and straddled him on the couch and smothered him with kisses.

The next morning over breakfast, Henry said he'd go ahead and wire the hotel and make travel reservations.

Opal's face dropped then showed her terror. She realized what *reservations* would entail. She hadn't even thought about it until then. "Oh, no, no, Henry, I can't ride on a stagecoach again. No, I, no, no, I just can't do it." Her tears started falling.

Henry reached out and took her hand in his. "It's all right, sweetie. I can rent a covered wagon. Would you be willing to do that? We can either sleep under the stars, if it's nice, or in the wagon if you prefer. No more than we need to take, we might even be able to just ride on horseback, but you wouldn't be able to take or bring back as much."

Opal considered the options. Horses would be faster, but they couldn't take as much. And what if it rained? No, the wagon sounded like the better choice.

"I think the wagon would be best. Do you think I'm being silly? Or too afraid?"

"No, not in the least. I hope one day you'll be able to ride the stage again, only because that means you'll be healed in your heart and not just your body. But, Opal, if that day doesn't come and you go your whole life not being able to ride on a stage-coach, that's fine, too. Nothing says you have to."

"I love you, Henry Tucker."

He smiled. "I love you, Opal Tucker."

"When I'm ready to ride the stage, I want you beside me."

"Yes, ma'am. I'll be there. All right, I'll wire the hotel and reserve the wagon today before I come home for lunch. We might have to spend two nights camping since the wagon won't be as fast as the stage—we won't be able to have fresh horses every two or three hours."

"That's fine with me. As long as I'm with you, I'm happy."

"All right, then. This evening after I come home, and before supper, I want us to get in some more target practice."

"I think I'll make a big pot of stew this morning, then I won't have to cook tonight. And we can practice as long as we want."

"Be warned, I won't fall for any more sucker bets."

She grinned at him.

———

HARRIET INVITED Opal to a morning visit with Amy and Evie Glover, the deputy's wife. Opal learned that the other three ladies had been meeting once every week or two, for the last three or four years, and naturally had become fast friends. Today, the visit was being hosted at Harriet's house.

"All right, ladies," Harriet said, "today, I have two different kinds of tea and coffee to go along with the cookies I made. One of the teas is an English brand that a friend back east sent to me. It's delicious and even better when you add my secret ingredient."

Amy and Evie laughed. Opal saw why when Harriet produced a bottle of whiskey.

"Your husbands don't mind if you drink?" Opal asked the ladies.

"No, they don't. We only have a little. What about Henry? Will he mind?"

"I don't think so. He brought me brandy after the Tatums' funeral. He has some whiskey and vodka at the house; we've just never drunk any of it before."

"Then we should be fine. It doesn't take much to doctor up a cup of tea," Harriet said.

Opal wanted to get started on a good foot. Amy was a dear friend already, but she'd only met Harriet and Evie a time or two. "Thank you for inviting me. I understand you three have been having these tea visits for quite a while."

"Yes, we have," Harriet said. "We started a few years ago—it was when Evie was brand new to the town. Remember the other night when I told you I had to carry a wooden spoon and Arthur used it on me in the kitchen of Mary's restaurant? Well, Evie had overheard me complain to Arthur that I was bored and didn't know anyone in town. I guess she took pity and invited me and Amy to visit her. And that's what started a tradition with us."

"It wasn't pity," Evie said. "I was new, too, and wanted to meet people." She winked at Harriet. "Well, maybe a little sympathy. The entire restaurant had just heard her get one powerful walloping."

"Oh, no! That must have been horrible for you, Harriet!"

The other three ladies laughed at their shared memory.

"You might think so, but, no, dear," Harriet said. "My big secret is that I love it when Arthur punishes me. I crave it. The rougher, the better. I act up just so he'll do it. I purposely instigated those thrashings at the restaurant."

Opal couldn't control her shock. It was one thing to enjoy a little spanking game, but real pain? With other people nearby? "I can't imagine that."

"Not many can, but it's how I am. I crave Arthur's dominance. I derive pleasure from being hurt, or what other people might think of as being abused, debased, humiliated. Now mind you, the public would only be privy to listening to the spankings take place. The other things—Arthur would never expose me to public ridicule in that way. That's all done in private."

Opal looked at Amy.

"It's true. Arthur is one of the sweetest men you'll ever meet. I was one of the people in the restaurant that day, when Evie asked Harriet to have tea, and I heard the spanking. I think

Harriet was genuinely embarrassed, but at the same time, she wanted it to happen. I've never once seen Arthur treat Harriet with anything but love and respect. But I've seen marks on her. She's shown us passive punishments, like when she's had to wear plugs or clamps. Needless to say, we don't speak of these things outside of our little tea group. I think many people would be scandalized and would ostracize them."

"Of course, I wouldn't betray a confidence."

"Thank you, dear," Harriet said. "Amy told us that you aren't a, um, skittish or easily offended person, and she said you'd fit into our circle quite well."

Opal looked at Amy again and smiled. "I suppose I should thank you again."

"Evie and I have benefitted from having Harriet as our friend. Perhaps you will, too."

"How so?" Opal asked.

Amy grinned at Opal and gave her a mischievous look. "By broadening your horizons. Opening your view of married relations. In essence, urging you to try new things. Be adventurous. Give up control. Jim and I have had a relationship rich with pleasures—diverse pleasures. Just hearing Harriet's experiences at these visits, has encouraged us to be, well, some people would say, most wicked and depraved. The beauty is those people don't know anything about it. But our husbands seem to enjoy the benefits."

"Amy, I stayed in your house all that time and I never knew."

"Of course not, Op," she said as she laughed. "These things are private! There were days when I was wearing a plug. There were times when Jim and I slipped out to the barn. Sometimes at night, he made me wear clamps."

"All right, now, wait. What are these plugs and clamps you keep talking about?"

"Ah! I can help there!" Harriet said. "I wanted to show you the results of the paddling I got this morning anyway."

"This morning! Why did you get one?"

"Because I asked for it," Harriet said, as though she should have known. "Let me show you," she said as she stood and turned around to face the opposite direction. Harriet began pulling up her skirt, revealing reddened skin on her thighs and cheeks where the word Obey was clearly readable even though it overlapped all over. The words on her thighs were easier to read because there were fewer.

"Oh my," Opal said. "Whoa! What's that?"

The other three laughed at her. "That's my plug. This is a large one. Imagine a darning egg with a flange on the end to keep it from going in all the way. That's the part you can see, that flange. It serves as a handle, too."

"You mean to tell me the rest of it is inside you? As big as a darning egg?"

"Yes, ma'am, it is. Let me go get my collection and show you."

Harriet was only gone for a quick moment, and Opal didn't have time to do anything but widen her eyes at Amy and Evie.

"They come in all sizes. Most are available through medical supply houses as rectal dilators, meant to stretch out people who have a physical problem. But Arthur has had the smithy make them for us before. He knows of a maker of glass ones, but we've never purchased one."

"Don't they... hurt?"

Harriet smiled and glanced at the other ladies before answering. "Well, they can. They must be inserted with a lubricant. I make my own out of menthol and very hot peppers. I like that sensation. Not everyone does. Most use a lotion or fat, like grease or butter or a salve. As for hurting, most do a little bit during insertion, but not so much once it's inside. Sitting can be a problem. Or a pain. If the plug is small enough, I don't even feel it until I move. Many times Arthur has made me wear them when we go out. Those times, it's not a punishment so much as a reminder of who has control over me. I find it to be a delicious secret. Other times, when it's a real punishment, we'll use a larger one that will hurt. He doesn't usually make me go anywhere with those in."

"How long can you leave them in?"

"Depends on the size. I've slept in small ones with no problem. The larger ones that are truly for punishment, not that long. From a few minutes to a few hours."

"They don't... stretch you out? I mean, that's their purpose, right?"

"Well, that's the medical purpose, but I can tell you, they don't work very well for that. You might stay stretched out for minutes, perhaps several minutes, but thus far, I've always gone back to the original shape and size eventually. Insertion seems to become easier with repetition, so I suppose that's a benefit. At least that's been my experience."

"Mine, too," Amy said.

"And these are punishments your husbands use on you?"

"Well," Evie said as she grinned, offering her own view. "Not always. Aaron introduced me to them when we were still newlyweds. My husband likes, um, relations back there, and the plugs help facilitate that."

Opal chose not to share her own experience she'd had with Henry. He'd indicated a strong desire to do that, but he hadn't pushed her. Maybe she'd check into getting some of these things as a surprise for him.

Harriet looked at her with narrowed eyes. "I see that look of contemplation on your face. You're new with us, so I won't ask you to share. But, I know that Clint stocks them and keeps them in the back room, out of view. I'll get you a set and let him think they're for us. No one else will know. How about that?"

For a brief second, Opal had the look of a small child who's just been caught doing something forbidden. But as seconds passed, the look turned into that of a curious woman eager to try something she'd never dreamed of before.

As Opal made her way home, she smiled at the thought of presenting the plugs to Henry on their honeymoon in Rawlins. What would he think of her? Yes, she'd definitely surprise him again.

Oh shoot! I forgot to find out about the clamps.

TEN

Opal enjoyed packing for their honeymoon. She started days in advance, just to make sure she included everything she wanted. Henry reminded her that there were even more stores in Rawlins, so it would be no problem if she forgot something.

She hid the dilator kit, having decided to add it at the last minute in case Henry looked through her suitcases. She kept reminding herself not to forget a suitable lubricant. She toyed with the idea of taking the *Obey* paddle, but she couldn't pack it early or Henry would realize something was amiss when their silent game was interrupted.

Opal planned their food for the trip. They could purchase food and supplies for the return trip home while they were there. She made up a cooking and baking schedule so she wouldn't be overburdened at the last minute with food preparations. Everything that could be made ahead of time would be.

THEY DIDN'T GET an early start on the date of their departure, but they weren't worried. Henry had already said they'd spend two nights on the road, and they were still in that timeframe.

The morning was spent gathering and packing all the things that hadn't been packed when he first brought the Prairie Schooner wagon home, the day before. Since the wagon was carrying a light load, no furniture or heavy equipment, they only needed two horses.

Opal had done last-minute cooking and those items were packed last. She finished packing her suitcase and a carpetbag at the last minute, with only a minor frustration that she hadn't been able to figure out where he'd hidden the paddle. It would have been fun to continue their hiding game on their trip, but it wasn't that important. She was excited, nonetheless.

Henry was excited, too, she could tell. He smiled even more than usual. Several times, he'd say something like, "All right, I have plenty of water for us and the horses, but I know of a few places on the way where the horses can drink. I should have enough. Can you think of anything else? Oh, I packed plenty of bedding, too. We might want to sit on pillows, you know. Those wagons aren't very comfortable. Can you think of anything else?"

Opal just smiled and reminded him they had food, clothing, and shelter and, technically, that was all they needed. The rest was just for convenience. It amused her to see this side of him, the side that was so eager to make this trip enjoyable for her. She was just as eager to make it a fun trip for him, too, but she didn't let it show.

Opal knew she had at least one thing that would surprise him. She hoped beyond hope that her friends had been honest with her and the new items wouldn't be painful for her when they tried them. She chuckled when she thought how Amy and Evie shared that both had been taken aback at just how uncomfortable and embarrassed they had both been when their husbands had initiated that kind of play and penetration the first time. Considering that Henry had seen to some of her intimate care even before they were married, she wasn't worried with the level of physical familiarity the toys would require.

They ate a quick lunch at the house and tidied the mess. Henry made sure to secure the lids to the milk and cream jugs because he wanted to take their perishables with them to have on the ride. Even though it would have still been good when they got back, he chose to put a hefty amount of butter in a sealed tin, because bread's just better with butter.

Following a sweet kiss for good luck, Henry whipped the reins and the horses moved. Opal grinned up at him with a look of adoration that made him melt. As they drove through town, most of the people who were outside saw them and waved. A few shouted for them to have a happy and safe trip. Opal realized that she might be the only person in town whom everyone knew, and it was simply because of the stagecoach massacre. They all seemed to have a soft spot for her, and she found that touching. She was becoming quite fond of a few of them, too.

"What's the first thing you want to do when we get to Rawlins?" she asked Henry.

He laughed. "What do you think? Fuck like animals."

She laughed back. "All right. And after that?"

"Scope out the best restaurants in town. Maybe find out about that book store and the playhouses and see what kind of entertainment's available."

"Sounds perfect to me. I just want it to be a relaxing time for both of us. I hope we don't even once find ourselves rushing to do things," Opal said.

"Agreed, I want the kind of honeymoon where we have no stress, long, cuddly bubble baths. Hot sex until we can't move our muscles anymore, plenty of sleeping in then more cuddling, and, well, you know what that leads to."

"I do. Do you think there may a day when we don't even leave the room?"

"Yes, ma'am. I wouldn't mind having a few like that."

"A day when we don't even put on clothes?"

"Absolutely. We'll have them leave food outside our door."

She was quiet a minute. "If I'm having that good a time, you may not be able to get me back home."

"I'll find a way."

They passed some time in silence, each lost in thought.

"Henry, do you ever wonder about what life is like in other parts of the world?"

"What do you mean?"

"Well, what does a marriage look like in Persia? Or Australia? What kind of relational dynamic do husbands and wives have? I've read that in some places wives don't have any rights and are treated no better than animals or other property. And in other places, husbands and wives, or men and women, are seen as equals. What kind of homes do they have on primitive islands, isolated from outsiders? What customs do they have that might be different than ours? That kind of thing."

"Interesting, and I don't know. I suspect that in European countries, they're interested in society and images. At least that's what I get from reading. I mean, some of those places are so populated, they don't have many open spaces like we have out here. I couldn't cite a source, but I bet they're just more formal. I also bet that although women are outwardly seen as treasures, they aren't always treated that way after marriage. Why? What do you think? What have you read?"

"My impression is much the same. I've read a lot of books, both fiction and non-fiction, and that's my sense of it. But what about other places you don't hear about as much? Like India?"

"Lots of people there, I know that. Probably not much

personal privacy. Lots of animals. I imagine in a lot of these places religion has a big influence on personal relationships."

"I'm sure that's true. Religion and perhaps government, too, in the settled areas. I wonder how many unknown peoples there are, say, on undiscovered islands, or hidden deep in the continents of Africa or South America? What must their lives be like? Their language? Or the people up in frozen regions? How do they entertain their children if it's too cold to go out and play?"

Henry turned to look at her. "I think I've married the most interesting woman in the whole world."

She dismissed that, laughing and waving her hand. "I doubt that."

"You're definitely the most interesting woman in my world." He smiled at her. "This conversation is making me think we'll never grow bored with each other. Why, this conversation alone could result in hours of discussion and not just banalities, substantive things." His voice lowered as it came from a sexy smirk. "I like that. I find that most stimulating, and not just in an intellectual sense."

"Are you saying the thought of undiscovered indigenous tribes makes you lustful?"

"Decidedly not. But having absorbing conversations with an educated, fascinating, enticing woman does. I may have to stop this wagon and have my way with you."

"Well, in that event, you should pull off the road first. We wouldn't want to get in anyone's way."

He threw back his head and gave a deep belly laugh. "Tonight's soon enough. I can be letting that steamy energy build up until then."

"Yes, I would be most appreciative of that," she quipped, giving him a sly look of her own.

They drove on for a while longer without much conversation. Opal thought about how she'd present him with the dilator plugs and what his reaction might be. She conjured up all kinds of scenarios and must have giggled or something because Henry asked her what she was thinking about. She didn't want to respond 'nothing', so she made up something. "I was just wondering if other couples have conversations like ours. I can't imagine Reverend Copperfield telling his wife he'll build up steamy energy so they can fuck like animals."

"Don't kid yourself. He's a man like any other." Henry laughed. "And all saints were once sinners. I had a friend who sometimes went with me to that brothel I told you about. He's a priest now."

"Oh, my! That is quite a turnaround," she said. She tilted her head. "So much of a turnaround, I can't imagine how one would do it. Once I had *carnal knowledge* of you, I only wanted more. No way I could stop!" She drew out the words *carnal knowledge*.

"Does my heart good to hear that, especially since I have every expectation of having more *carnal knowledge*." He drew out the words, too. "To tell the truth, I've never understood how priests can do that. It must be some strong religious calling to make a man, or a woman for that matter, turn away from a biological imperative. I don't know how they can ignore it."

"I'm glad we're Methodist. I understand they encourage marital relations."

He gave his head a nod. "Damn right."

A SMALL WAVE of unease passed over Opal; she knew they must be nearing the way station at Williston. When she saw it in the distance, she asked Henry to pull over when they got there. She needed to take a break, and besides, she wanted to somehow pay homage or show respect to Mr. Birdwhistle.

Henry stopped the horses just off the road and helped Opal down. The attendant saw them and came over to greet them.

"Howdy folks, how are you this fine day? Name's Will Brennan." He held out his hand for Henry to shake. "Don't get many visitors. Just the stage folks, and don't have time to talk to any of them, they're in such a hurry to get back on the road."

""Henry Tucker, and this is my wife, Opal."

"How do you do?" they both said.

"You folks headed to Rawlins? Or parts farther out?"

"Yes, Rawlins," Opal answered. "Actually, we're on our honeymoon."

Mr. Brennen perked up. "Well, congratulations to ye both. I guess you're just taking a rest here 'afore you head on, then."

"Yes, sir, that's right. My wife wanted to stop here. The last time she was this way, the station master before you had just been killed. I think she wanted to take time to honor him."

A shadow crossed Brennan's face and his brow furrowed. "That was you, little lady? I heard a young woman survived. I'm sure happy you made it. And I'm real happy your life took a happy turn. I wish I had a place to invite you in to chat, but I only got a stump to sit on there in the lean-to. My cabin's over yonder, but it ain't barely big enough for me."

"Oh, that's fine, Mr. Brennan," Opal said. "I just wanted to show Henry how things happened. There was another man on the stage with us who traveled this route often; he said Mr. Birdwhistle was a friendly man."

"He was; he surely was. I knew him fairly well. He lost his wife about four years ago, then he took this job to get away from the memories. Their only child died as a baby. I remember him saying the only thing that got him through the passing of his wife was knowing that she was with their baby Noah now."

Opal smiled. "And he's with both of them now, a family made whole again." She looked toward the lean-to, where the fresh horses stood, and started walking. "His body was right there," she said as she pointed. "Face down, his head was toward the horses. He must have been running for cover, or maybe running to get his gun, when they shot him in the back."

Neither of the men spoke.

"I understand ye wuz hurt pretty bad, Miz Tucker," Mr. Brennen finally said.

"I was shot twice and lost a lot of blood. But thank the good Lord, I healed."

"Well, ma'am, I do thank the good Lord for that. Do ye know if they ever found them sons o' guns?"

Henry answered for her, "Not yet, but there are leads, and several men are looking. Opal was able to tell them what she remembered."

"Well, then I'm double glad ye lived through it. Otherwise, they probably wouldn't have anything to go on."

Henry nodded. "That's exactly what I thought. Opal, we should probably head on now. We've still got a little way before we stop for the night."

"All right. But I do need a quick stop. You two can keep talking while I find some bushes across the road."

"Yes, ma'am," Brennan said. "We'll do just that. I sure wish I had better facilities for ye."

She'd already turned around and begun walking and waved her hand as if to dismiss the thought. "What nature provided is more than adequate."

"THERE'S a spot up ahead where I want to camp for the night. It has a bridge over a creek that cuts into the woods, about a hundred yards off the road. The creek makes a bend and there's a clearing by it that's completely hidden from this road."

"That sounds perfect. But you know there are no other souls out here on this road. We could have complete privacy if we camped right there." She pointed at a spot just beside the road. "Matter of fact, you could probably just stop here in the road and make camp," she joked.

"I could. But for what I have in mind, you'll probably want to be secluded." He winked at her.

"Good. Something about seeing that horse station and learning more about Mr. Birdwhistle, I don't know, I feel the need to do something that celebrates life."

"Don't forget, I've been building up steamy energy all afternoon. Remember? So we can fuck like animals? Is that enough of a celebration for you?"

She gave her head a shake and echoed his own words from earlier in the day, "Damn right."

Henry turned off the road about thirty yards short of the bridge and angled toward the woods where the creek disappeared. He pulled in far enough for the wagon to be hidden and stopped. Opal stood and stretched then let Henry help her down. He pulled her into his arms and hugged hard, not letting her go for quite a while. Finally, he loosened his embrace and bent to kiss her. It wasn't a chaste kiss.

"Henry!" she said when he pulled away, and his name sounded like a moan. "Careful. We still need to make camp and fix supper and tend the horses."

"I know. Couldn't help it, though."

"I like that," she said, tracing her hand over his fullness. "Tell you what, you take care of the horses while I find some firewood and get a fire going."

"Sounds like a good plan. Stay where I can see you. It's starting to get dark."

"I need to pee first. Then I'll stay where you can see me."

"I've seen it all already, swee' pea. Stay where I can see you.

Opal started to flash him a peeved look, then she realized he was right.

She looked around the campsite and saw where a fire had burned before. Someone had encircled the spot with rocks. There were enough fallen twigs and branches in the clearing to get the fire going, but she knew they'd need more for the night.

"I need to leave your sight so I can gather more wood before dark."

"All right. Sing."

"What?"

"*Camptown Races*. Sing, so I can hear where you are."

"Oh," she said. "I can do that." She chose not to ask him why she couldn't have done that while she peed.

So she sang. When she had the wood stacked conveniently near the fire, she started in on supper. It would be mostly a cold supper, but she fried some ham, so they'd have hot meat to go with the bread and butter, cheese, and pickled okra. She poured them each a cup of milk. It was still cool but not cold. Henry tossed his bread into the ham skillet to get it toasty.

When their meal was finished, Opal produced a bag of cookies.

"If I'd known you had those, I'd have been eating them on the way!"

"I know. Then we wouldn't have any for dessert now."

"I ought to give you a good hidin' for that. Depriving me of cookies, is that any way to treat your husband?" There was a flirty quality to his voice.

"Are you implying I don't know how to treat my husband?"

"I'm implying that perhaps you need a reminder."

He reached under the horse quilt they sat on and produced the paddle.

Opal gasped in surprise and her mouth opened. She recovered and looked at him suspiciously. "No wonder I couldn't find it," she said, grinning at him.

"Well, darlin', I owe you a hidin'. I think you need to take your clothes off now."

"Any possibility I can bargain my way out of it?" she asked as she stood and began undressing.

"Nope," he said as he stood and removed his gun belt and belt. "But you might convince me to go easy on you."

"What'll it take?"

"This burden's on you, darlin'. Make me an offer. What do you think I would like?"

"You like it when I suck you."

He let out a whistle. "I do like that. I like that a lot. What else you got?"

"That's not enough for you to go light on me?"

"A little bit, it is. But you know, I can probably swing this baby pretty hard. You might need to offer me more."

"All right. You like it when I get on top."

"Ah, yes, I do." He gave a chin jut and grinned. "You're gettin' there."

She threw her remaining clothes on the ground in mock frustration. "And you like it when I talk dirty."

"You drive a hard bargain, darlin', but you beat me." He grinned as he showed her the paddle. "I only want to do it hard enough to see your name show up. See this? I took it to Angus and had him put your name on the other side."

Opal chuckled. "I should have known. But I have a condition, too. Take your clothes off."

"Oh, all right." He shucked his clothes and tossed them near hers.

"Now, how do you want me?"

He looked at her and with twinkling eyes and a lascivious grin. "Desperately."

"You know what I mean. Bending over? Touching my toes? Standing up? Hugging a tree? On the ground? Bent over while you hold me under your arm? Over your knee while you're sitting on that fallen tree?"

He laughed at the way she rattled off the choices. "Have you been fantasizing about this? Sounds like you've given it some thought."

"I may have."

He folded his arms over his chest. "Touch yourself while I decide. Like you were doing when I walked in on you."

She did, and as she let herself become more absorbed in it, she began to become aroused and sway and undulate as she moved. Her eyes closed and she seemed to bask in the cool of the breeze and the heat of the fire. Henry thought the sight of her dancing erotically in the firelight was the most sensual and provocative thing he'd ever seen.

He watched until he couldn't any more. He threw the paddle on the ground by their clothes.

"I can't wait, darlin'. All those things we talked about can wait. I have to have you now. Right now."

He pushed her forcefully to her knees, on the blanket, then pushed her forward on her elbows.

"I built up a powerful need, darlin', just watching you move."

"Good," she panted, nearly breathless. "I can't wait, either. I want you to come at me like a runaway locomotive."

THE NEXT MORNING, they were awake before the sun, but neither of them wanted to leave the other's arms, nestled in their cozy quilt cocoon on the ground.

At one point in the night, Opal had gotten a little agitated in her sleep but hadn't awakened. She had wakened Henry, though, and he was worried she'd had another nightmare.

"Did you sleep well, darlin'? Any bad dreams?"

"I slept like a happy, full-bellied baby. The cool night air maybe? I liked having the stars overhead and your arms around me. How about you?"

"Cool night air, my hind foot. I slept like a baby because you wore the everlovin' fuck out of me last night." He tightened his arms around her, no longer concerned that she'd had a bad dream. "I've never seen anything as beautiful as you dancing naked by that fire. It's burned into my brain and I imagine it'll be my favorite memory until the day I die."

"I've never done anything like that before. I wouldn't have if you hadn't told me to touch myself. It was... I don't know, like I got lost in the sensations and couldn't keep from moving to my own rhythm."

"So, do you think dancing by the fireplace will make you do that, or are we going to have to camp out in the backyard every night from now on?"

Opal laughed at him.

THEY DOUSED THE FIRE, cleaned up the campsite and packed everything away after a hearty breakfast. Henry made sure the rest of the cookies would be within his reach on the wagon, as was the remainder of the jar of milk. They'd let it sit in the creek water overnight and it was nice and cold.

He took the reins in his hands then turned to Opal. "Let's

have another kiss for good luck, darlin'; it sure did work for us yesterday."

There was a slightly overcast sky and the temperature was comfortably cool; it was perfect traveling weather. Opal hummed and sometimes Henry joined in or whistled.

"I was thinking about our conversation from yesterday," he said. "You know what makes me curious? Thinking about undiscovered people who've had no contact with anyone outside their own community. No traders, no missionaries, completely left to their own devices. For example, what do they do for clothes?"

"Probably not much—most would be in warm climes, right? Leaves, as in Adam and Eve style? Oh, I bet they learned to weave strips of whatever trees or plants or vines that are available and pliable."

"Wouldn't take much, I imagine. Nobody's taught them to be ashamed of their bodies, so whatever they wore would be for comfort and practicality."

"And how do women handle their monthly times?"

"They probably don't do anything. Just wash when they can," he answered. "Animal skins, maybe? Who knows?"

"Isn't it amazing to think there's a whole big world out there we know nothing about? We're all so preoccupied with our own little worlds that we miss the big picture. What must God think of us?"

"I wouldn't even pretend to know that, little darlin'. But it seems like we ought to be nicer to each other, doesn't it, when you think about it like that."

Opal agreed, and they both sat in silent contemplation for a while.

A LITTLE LATER, Opal realized she recognized the area. She got a little light-headed and felt nauseated for a moment before the feeling went away. "Henry, please pull off the road. Right here. Now. I want to get down."

"All right."

He helped her down. "There are some thick bushes over there you can use. I'll go over here."

"No, it's not that."

Henry watched as she found a long, sturdy stick and went back to the road a few yards ahead of their wagon. Opal looked around, as if to get her bearings, then nodded almost impercep-tibly to herself. She began to draw a huge rectangle outline in the dirt road. When she drew four thick, shorter lines outside the rectangle, one at the front and back of each long side, he realized they represented wheels.

"You're drawing the stagecoach, aren't you? Is this where it happened, sweetheart?"

"Yes. I want to show you."

She went to one end of the rectangle, the end closest to him, and extended the lines as though lengthening the rectangle. "This is where the driver and the man riding shotgun sat."

Opal drew a line protruding from the driver's seat, then she drew representations of four horses in front of the line. Henry knew the line must be the wagon tongue. She stood back and looked at her work and nodded. Then, she went back inside the rectangle and drew three boxes going across it. The middle one was shorter. "These are the benches we sat on."

Henry had ridden in countless stagecoaches in his life, but he felt as though he was seeing them freshly through her eyes.

"On that day, I sat here, the window seat." She drew a circle inside the bench rectangle. She drew another circle a few inches away. "Mrs. Tatum sat here. She had on a pretty yellow dress that day. I complimented her on it, and she said she bought the fabric and trims from a street vendor in the city of Bangkok, in Siam." Opal smiled at the memory.

She drew a third circle. "This was Mr. Tatum, here, by the other window. Oh, I guess I should indicate where the door was. The opening was about from here," she drew a short line to demark one side of the door, "to about here."

She stepped back and drew a circle on the middle bench, near where her circle was. "This was where Mr. Keppler sat. He was the only one on the middle bench. He straddled it so he wouldn't have his back to anyone. The Deans sat over here. Mr. Dean was by this window, his wife in the middle, and their daughter by the other window." She drew all the circles as she spoke.

Opal paused in her narration and looked away, looking at nothing in particular. "We were having a lively conversation about people with funny names. Mr. Keppler started it when he told us about Mr. Birdwhistle. We all knew it isn't nice to make fun of someone's name, but we couldn't help laughing at a few of them. Then came the knock on that wall. He said to get our guns if we had them."

She pointed in the air above the outline of her bench as though a physical coach stood there. "I was scared, Henry, but not scared for my life. I expected we'd be robbed of our valuables and they'd take the money Keppler mentioned, but that we'd soon be on our way. I even felt a little smug because I had pinned some paper money to my petticoat, and they wouldn't get that or the brooch I wore under my dress." She smiled ruefully at him. "And those were just things, Henry, things. Things I now know aren't important at all."

She moved to stand by her circle in the spot she'd stand if she were about to sit down. "There were shouts and some gunshots and the stage stopped too fast. It bounced us all around and even when we were stopped, we could tell from inside the coach that it rattled the horses. The door burst open and the one called Red Eye stuck his rifle inside and demanded our money and jewelry. The other man, Jed, was right beside him, but I only got fleeting glimpses of him, when he'd step into view for a second. But I did see his gun because he kept his gun hand in the doorway much of the time."

Opal made a motion with her hand and pointed a finger vaguely in Henry's direction. "I just realized they all wore kerchiefs over their faces. I don't think they meant to kill us at all. They were hiding their faces so we couldn't identify them later."

Henry nodded in understanding.

"We were nervous and fumbled with our things, but we all handed over our bags and wallets. I remember Mrs. Tatum had difficulty removing her wedding rings. We heard shooting outside. They got both the driver and the man beside him. I think that's when we heard the Englishman—he'd gotten the money box. Mr. Tatum tried to calm us. He told us to hand over our valuables. Jed stepped closer to the door and I got a good look at his hand when he stuck it in. Another voice outside said they needed to leave in a hurry. That's when Mr. Keppler stood up and shot Red Eye. Then Jed shot Keppler and he fell onto me. His chin hit my shoulder; I think that's why he didn't fall down to the floor."

Henry noticed the slight shudder that went through Opal.

"The Englishman gave orders to kill all of us. Mr. Dean stood up right here to shoot at Jed, but Jed was quicker. Mr. Dean fell onto me, too, on my right side. That's the last thing I remember until I came to later."

"Opal, darlin', I'm amazed you've been able to remember this much."

She shrugged. "I didn't at first, but it's come back to me in bits and pieces."

Henry wanted to take her in his arms, but he didn't want to distract her from this reenactment. She might mention something else that could help the law, and more importantly, this might help exorcise her demons and allow her heart and mind to heal. Elliott had told them to listen if the time ever came when she wanted to speak about it.

"What happened when you came to, sweetie?"

Opal closed her eyes and began to speak slowly. "I had to fight for my breath, and I panicked. I realized the two men had fallen on me. When I tried to push them off, I found I'd been shot, too. It hurt to breathe, and I couldn't use my left arm. Keppler fell on the floor here in front of Mrs. Tatum. Dean was right here. I had to move him a little more to get my canteen. I was too weak to stand and had to sit on the bench and work my feet over to that side. I couldn't help but put my feet on Mr. Dean. I scooted on down the bench to the end. I was losing blood and already dizzy. It took a long time to get down the steps, and it hurt."

Opal stepped across the rectangle, retracing her steps on that day. She stood outside the rectangle. "I tried to lean on the wagon for support. Red Eye was on the ground here. I didn't want to step on him, but I had to when I made my way to the horses after I got the coach door closed."

She made her way closer to the outlines of the driver's seat and the horses.

"The man who rode shotgun was against the front wheel. It looked almost as though he sat there on purpose, like he was leaning against a tree, except he seemed pinched under the wheel, leaning forward. The horses were fretful, but the body under the wheel kept them from being able to take off. I'd heard they can be calmed by voices, so I tried to talk soothingly. I couldn't think of what to say, so I sang."

Opal closed her eyes again, began singing, and opened them again a few lines into the song.

"COME, *thou fount of every blessing.*
Tune my heart to sing Thy grace.
Streams of mercy, never ceasing,
Call for songs of loudest praise.
Teach me some melodious sonnet.
Sung by flaming tongues above.
Praise the mount,
I'm fixed upon it,
Mount of Thy redeeming love.
Here I raise mine Ebenezer.
Hither by Thy help, I'm come.
And I hope, by Thy good pleasure.
Safely to arrive at Home."

HENRY WAS JUST ABOUT to start singing softly along with her, but she stopped and looked directly at him. Tears streamed down her face. "That verse talks about home, meaning Heaven. It didn't mean Heaven to me that day. I sang it like a prayer, asking God to get me home to you. That prayer sustained me all the rest of the way."

His tears fell, too, but he resisted the urge to run over and take her in his arms. He knew she needed this.

Opal turned back to the dirt outlines. "The reins had fallen to the ground, and since I couldn't bend and crawl, I used the driver's rifle to pull them to me. When I got hold of them, I stood about here and pulled back. I'm not sure how, but I got the horses to back up just enough to free the man's body from under the wheel."

Opal put her hand in the air on the imaginary wheel. "The first time I thought I might die was when I had to get up on that driver's seat. Nothing ever hurt as bad, Henry. My side and my shoulder throbbed in pain and I was bleeding so much, I was weak and dizzy. I thought my heart would beat out of my body. I had to climb up this wheel until I could heave myself over onto the bench. I don't know how long it took. I finally got up there but almost passed out. Once I got in the seat, I had to sit a good long while just to catch my breath and let my heartbeat calm down. That's when I ripped up my petticoats and wrapped my side. From then on, all I could do was keep going and pray for an army of angels to get me home to you."

"I sure am glad He sent you those angels," Henry said through tears that had been slowly but steadily falling as he listened to her.

Opal walked to him, into his arms, and they stayed that way for the longest time until she pulled away. "You know most of the rest. The other time I was afraid I would die was when I had to leave Williston with tired horses. I was so afraid I wouldn't make it. I was so weak and faint and in so much pain."

"But you did make it, Opal," he said as he hugged her again, rubbing her back.

She pulled away, smiling as she took a deep breath and squared her shoulders. "Don't let this go to your head, Henry Tucker, but knowing what I know how, I'd have endured twice as much, as long as it meant coming home to you."

Henry was overcome by so many emotions that he couldn't focus on any one in order to make a comment. His lip quivered a little and he held up his arms for another hug.

She rose up to kiss his cheek. "All right, *now* I need to use the bushes. Then we can be on our way, and a few miles up the road, we can stop to fix lunch."

OPAL'S MOOD was much brighter after sharing that experience with Henry. Maybe she felt she didn't have to bear the burden of that day's memories on her own shoulders anymore. He wondered if this would have a cathartic effect on her; he hoped it would.

Henry's mood was more mixed. He thought he understood more clearly how much horror she had endured that day. Her pain was far deeper than he had realized, and he felt guilt for not having understood the depth of it.

When they passed through the tiny settlement of Cooper's Gap, she insisted on stopping and visiting the family who ran the station. They, of course, knew of the tragedy and as soon as the station master's wife saw Opal, she recognized her. Mrs. Cooper insisted upon feeding them, and after initially expressing sympathies over the tragedy, she kept the conversation light.

That night as they lay down on their pallet under the clear starry sky, they talked. They talked of their house, their future family, their neighbors, Angus and his paddles, Opal's new nephew, the playhouses in Rawlins, and how many new books would fit into her bookshelves. They talked and giggled and laughed for hours until sleep found them.

ELEVEN

Opal had only been in Rawlins once, and then it was only for a couple of hours. She'd only seen the short distance between the railroad station and the stagecoach line, and they were on the outskirts of town.

Henry had been in town enough times to generally know his way around, so he played tour guide as they rode in, to the extent of his knowledge. He pointed out restaurants he'd dined in and the ones he'd like to visit again.

Opal spotted a saloon on a seedier-looking side street and playfully asked him if he'd been in it. He hesitated and that told her his answer.

"You have been in there!" she said as she laughed and swatted his arm. "I won't ask how many times or how many fancy ladies entertained you."

"What can I say? A man away from home in a strange town... he gets lonely."

She stretched up to whisper in his ear, "You won't get lonely on this trip. I have plans."

A big smile stretched across his face. "So do I, darlin'. So do I."

IT WAS the fanciest and most modern hotel in town. Henry hadn't ever stayed in it, but he'd heard it was the best one. The sumptuous lobby was warm and inviting, with clusters of small tables surrounded by overstuffed and comfortable-looking chairs and loveseats.

They were ushered to the honeymoon suite and given a brief tour of it by a neatly dressed bellhop. Henry tipped him and the man walked out, closing the door behind himself.

Opal spun around the room then dropped onto the bed.

"Look at this place, Henry! I'm never going to want to leave. Cold *and hot* running water. Hot running water! Just think if we had that at home, in both the kitchen and bathroom! Can we have that, Henry? Please?"

He laughed at the pleading look in her eyes. "This isn't fair. Do you have any idea what it takes to get hot running water? We'll have to make a few changes to the house. We'll have to make a place for a boiler and figure out the best way to keep the water heated. I think they use gas here. You do realize, don't you, that we would be the first house in Big Rock to have hot running water? The hotel doesn't even have it."

"Think how convenient it would be." Her big, hopeful eyes reminded him of the puppy he had as a child.

"Damn. You know I can't say no to you."

Opal jumped up from the bed and on Henry, wrapping her arms and legs around him. She smothered his face in little kisses. "I just can't even think of all the ways I can show you my appreciation," she said.

"Will I get to select some of those ways?"

"Yes, sir."

"Oh, darlin', you know how I like that *sir* thing. Too bad I didn't pack that riding crop."

"Hey, don't get ahead of yourself here. Maybe I should wait until after we have hot running water before I should show all this appreciation."

"As long as you still plan to keep me from being lonely on this trip."

"I brought a surprise," she said, looking up at him flirtatiously.

"A surprise? And when do you plan to give it to me?"

"I think I'll wait a day or two."

"Are you going to give me a hint?"

"No, sir."

He smirked and tilted his head. "Not even a teeny-tiny, little hint?"

"No, sir," she said. "But I'm certain you'll like it, so it'll be well worth waiting for."

"All right, but after that build up, if I don't like it, your ass is mine."

"It might be anyway," she said as she winked and turned to walk into the bathroom.

AFTER A LAZY AFTERNOON spent mostly in a long, soaking bath, they went downstairs to the hotel restaurant for an early supper. It was well-appointed and featured a varied menu, with several foreign dishes that the waiter had to describe. They made their selections and Henry ordered a bottle of wine.

"All right," Opal said, "tell me what you want us to do while we're in town."

He scooted his chair closer to her and leaned in. "It's a honeymoon. I just want to fuck you senseless. Anything else we do is your choice."

"Good. That falls right in line with my plans. We can start tonight. What do you think?"

"I'll even be willing to forego dessert so we can get started."

"I want dessert, but I'll eat it quickly. Will that work?"

"It will."

They kept up the banter until their appetizers were served.

"Where can we find out about the current plays and any other entertainment?"

"At the front desk, most likely."

"Good. I want to ask about the best places to buy dresses and shoes, too. Isn't there anything you'd like to shop for while we're in a big city?"

"I guess I could check in to the plumbing supplies we'll need for hot running water."

Opal chuckled. "Well, if you think they won't have it all in Big Rock, then by all means, let's get it here. There's plenty of room in the wagon, you know."

"Well, I'll be," Henry said as he stood and waved someone over.

Opal turned and saw Reed and Deacon Snow walking toward them. She'd met them a time or two and knew they were working on the stage massacre case. "How long have you men been here in town?" she asked.

"Two or three days," Deacon said.

"I take it you're here on business," Henry said, and everyone around the table knew he meant *are you here looking for the killers*.

"We've had leads that brought us here. We suspect there may be a fifth man who was in on it. It looks like he's been on another heist with them. They hit a bank over at Percy and were trailed here by a couple of federal marshals, but they lost them. We've got men at the train and stage offices, to make sure they don't hop one of them. All roads leading out of town have men posted, too. There are men camped out in surrounding areas. Unless they managed to slink out into the night in the woods or vanish into thin air, they're here in town."

Henry sensed the tension that came upon Opal and he took her hand. "It's all right, sweetie, it sounds like they're almost in custody already."

"Mrs. Tucker," Reed said, "I don't believe you're in danger. We'll get 'em."

She managed a polite smile. "I know you will."

Henry wanted to change the subject. "Aren't you two from Rawlins?"

"Sure are. Grew up here. Why?" Reed asked.

"Opal wants to know where the best dress shops and milliners are, and we both want to know where the best restaurants are."

"We can help with restaurants, but you're on your own for everything else."

The men pulled up chairs and gave Henry a solid list of places with excellent food. They left when the newlyweds' entrees were brought out.

Opal picked at her food. "I can't believe I picked a time to come here when those killers would be in town."

"Maybe the fates want you to be here when they're caught, so you can see for yourself. Or at least be in the same town, so you can read about it in the papers."

"All right, that's a positive aspect I can believe," she conceded.

"And I'm not averse to staying inside the whole time and not even going out."

She couldn't keep from smiling a little. "You might get tired of the food downstairs."

"Darlin', as long as you're giving me sexy surprises and

keeping me from 'being lonely', I'll eat scrambled eggs three times a day."

"We'll see about tomorrow, but tonight, I'm glad we're staying in. For more than one reason."

THE NEXT MORNING after a breakfast downstairs, they stopped at the front desk to inquire about shopping. Opal was glad a woman was behind the desk.

They walked back upstairs with the names and addresses of several shops. Opal was still reluctant to get out on the streets, but Henry convinced her that a women's dress shop was the last place they'd run into any bad men. Since three of the stores were nearby, that clinched the deal for her. They went shopping.

Henry proved to be entertaining company and totally got her mind off the criminal element in town. They went to the largest store first, and it ended up being all they had time for in one day. She hadn't planned to purchase undergarments or nightgowns, but he selected some for her. He selected some she considered scandalous.

As they headed into the hotel, Henry said, "I think I'll order dinner brought up to our room tonight. Whatever their special is, topped off with that gooey chocolate dessert served with vanilla custard. What do you think?"

"I like that a lot."

He knew she was grateful not to have to leave the hotel, especially at night.

She *was* grateful. So much so that she almost decided to share her surprise, but she chose to wait until the next night. They enjoyed a good enough time without trying any new things.

The next morning, they slept in again, each saying they'd better not start getting used to it or they'd have a hard time adjusting when they got back home. They ate a leisurely breakfast then went back upstairs to freshen up before hitting another store on Opal's list.

This one was a dress store and milliner, and they even had a counter with shoes and boots. Opal felt she was in shopping heaven.

Henry kept it fun, because whenever their sales woman was out of earshot, he whispered funny comments about almost all of the hats, especially the feathered ones.

"You'd better be careful wearing this one. Harry Peterson's so blind, he'll think you're a giant turkey."

"I could hold you upside down and sweep the floor with you."

"That's got so many feathers, I won't know whether to fuck you or pluck you."

The last one made her laugh so hard, she had tears in her eyes, and Henry managed to stand there with a completely straight and innocent face when the saleslady came back in.

"Would you like to try on some of those hats on that rack? They're the very latest, inspired by the fashions of London and Paris."

"Oh, no, thank you," Opal said, recovering her equilibrium. "They're far too grand for the small town where we live. But I would like to try on some more modest ones to wear on Sundays."

"Oh, yes, I can show you several I think are more practical and still very pretty and fashionable. I know we'll find some you'll love."

They did find a couple that she and Henry both liked.

On the walk back to the hotel, they passed a bakery. Opal

wanted to go in and try some sweet treats and have tea. They were enjoying themselves, and Henry sensed that Opal's tensions and fears were lightening up. This was confirmed when, on the walk back to the hotel, she said she was ready to go out to eat at a restaurant for dinner. "I don't want to go too far, though, if you don't mind."

"Sweetie, I'm proud of you. We'll find one that's close."

She grinned. "I might even give you your surprise tonight when we get back from supper."

He grinned back. "Well, all-righty then. Let's find a very close restaurant, with a fast cook. A place where they want you to leave so fast, they push you out the door with dessert wrapped up in a bag in your hand."

AS THEY WALKED up the stairs to their room upon their return from dinner, Henry put his arm around Opal and spoke in a low voice. "All right, when we get in the room, should I go ahead and get naked? Should you? Should we both? Or is that part of it? Will you undress me?"

Opal burst out laughing. "You've been thinking about this all during dinner, haven't you?"

"Oh my Lord, yes. It was all I could do not to mention it there."

"I surely do hope I haven't gotten your expectations so high I can't live up to them. I'll be awfully disappointed."

He gave her a sly, sideways glance. "We could always play with the paddle, you know. We still haven't done that."

Once inside, Opal put down her bag and Henry took his wallet out of his pocket and set his jacket over the back of one of the chairs.

"What now?" he asked.

"Since it's turned off cooler, maybe you should start a fire in the fireplace."

"Good idea. Will you dance naked in front of it for me later?"

"I might."

When Henry bent to put the wood in the fireplace, he laughed when he saw the paddle sitting in the kindling bucket provided by the hotel. He stacked three pieces of wood and used some kindling and bits of paper to get the fire going.

He stood up and turned to find that Opal had gone into the bathroom, so he went ahead and took off his shirt, boots, and socks. He turned down the bed linens, so they wouldn't be in the way later, then went back to stand by the mantle.

He caught his breath when she walked out with two brightly wrapped packages in her hand. It wasn't the packages that took his breath away. She was wearing the briefest of the nightwear he had purchased for her. It was a short, loose gown that almost revealed more than it covered. The delicate shoulder straps were thin, and the bodice was low. So low, in fact, that it exposed much of the tops of her breasts, barely covering her nipples. The flirty, ruffled hemline came only inches below her bottom, exposing most of her legs to his view.

He gave a satisfied and admiring whistle. "Darlin'. Just. Darlin'. I can't even think of what to say about how delicious you look. And I thought you looked good in front of that fire the other night. Come on over here."

It was the reaction she wanted. She knew he'd like the gown. She liked it, too—the way the soft, thin fabric clung to her curves, made her feel feminine and even attractive.

She handed him the first little package. "It's a two-part gift."

"All right, that sounds good," he said, smiling. "Two surprises are always better than one."

He eyed her and purposely opened it very slowly, building up the excitement. A confused look came on his face.

"Creamy salve? You gave me a tin of creamy salve? What, does my manhood have sores on it or something?"

She laughed as she handed him the other package. "I said it was a two-part gift."

Henry gave her a questioning look and opened the second package. "Whoa." Then he laughed. "Well, darlin', you definitely did surprise me with this one." He looked up at her. "I'm surprised you even know what these are."

She shrugged and grinned. "Harriet."

"That explains it a little more."

"I'd never heard of them. Evie and Amy... oh well, I probably shouldn't say that. But, Harriet got a set for me so I wouldn't have to be embarrassed in front of Clint. So... I guess you're familiar with them? And you know how to use them?"

"I told you my past isn't pure."

"Is this another whorehouse story?"

"Yes. In Chinatown, in San Francisco. I'll have to take you out to San Francisco someday. Anyway, they sold a lot of these things. Other toys, too."

"Toys?"

"Sex toys. Things to play with during sex."

"I never dreamed of such."

He laughed. "It pleases me to hear that. I'd like to be the one to introduce you to a few toys, but it sounds like Harriet may beat me to it."

"This was all she talked about. Oh, wait! She mentioned clamps but didn't say what they were. What are clamps?"

"Nipple clamps, I imagine."

She instinctively reached up to protect her nipples. "Wouldn't that hurt?"

"They certainly can if you want them to."

She looked at him questioningly, watching him pull each of the three plugs out of the box and examine them.

"Would you want them to?"

"Maybe, just a little bit." He made a mental note to devise some homemade clamps when he got home.

"Why?" She eyed him, still holding her nipples.

"It all enhances sensation. Remember that woman who liked spanking? She loved a little pain. Some people like a lot. You know what?" he said, holding up a plug in front of her. "I dang near bought a set of these, but I didn't have a woman in my life then. Had no idea when I'd be able to use 'em. Darlin', this may be the best present you ever gave anybody."

"Good, I'm glad. Now you won't have to pull out the paddle."

"Maybe, maybe not. Maybe I'd like to give you a surprise."

He pulled her to him in a kiss, still holding the smaller plug. "I'm going to enjoy putting this inside you," he whispered. "Undress me the rest of the way."

She unbuttoned his britches and his drawers, lowered them down his legs, and held them while he stepped out. When she stood, she threw them over the chair with his shirt and started caressing his hardness with both hands. Then she knelt down again.

A few moments later, Henry guided them to the bed. "You gave me weak knees again, darlin'. Give me a minute, then I want to turn all my attention to you and this body I find myself dreaming of night and day. Here, let's get this nightgown off. It's served its purpose for now."

Henry set the toy items on the nightstand and began touching Opal all over. His touch was whisper light and fleeting until she begged for more. He gave her more, letting his mouth take one nipple. He teased it with his breath, tongue and teeth until she started the purrs and mewling sounds he loved to hear, then he gave equal treatment to her other tip. He teased it with his hand, squeezing and flicking then squeezing again.

Opal's hips began to undulate, and his other hand drifted down to her cleft. He gave a satisfied moan when he found it soaking wet. "Turn over on your tummy."

She did. He rubbed his hand all over her back, bottom and thighs, thinking how much he adored this view. He concentrated solely on her bottom for a while, delving down into her crease so she could get accustomed to his touch there. He rubbed up and down it then rubbed little circles over and around her little crinkled rosette.

"How does that feel, darlin'?" he asked.

"Foreign at first, but I'm getting used to it. It's nice."

"Good. I want you to enjoy it."

"So you aren't trying to inflict pain this time?" she asked.

"No, not this time. This is purely for fun. A new sensation for you," he replied.

"Did you ever try it on yourself?"

He paused, not knowing where she was going with this. "No."

"Hmm."

"Hmm, what?"

"I might be interested in seeing how you like the sensation. What do you think about that?" she teased.

"Never considered it before. I'd definitely need a drink or two first."

She chuckled. "We can do that."

Henry opened the tin and dipped his finger in the gooey cream. He spread her apart with his left hand. The goo was cold and made Opal giggle when he touched her with it and resumed the circling motion.

"You all right?"

"Yes. It's cold."

He smiled. "I'll try to warm it next time."

"What if I don't like it?" she worried.

"You will. Does it still feel good?"

She paused. "Yes," she whispered.

He quickly inserted the tip of his finger before she could react. He continued the gentle slow circles just inside her. "How about now?"

"It's almost... nice."

Henry repositioned himself so he could reach her with his other hand. He nudged her legs apart and began rubbing her cleft, including her little pearl. He extracted his finger long enough to get more of the lubricant, then he inserted two fingers. He worked them all around, spreading them apart some and then keeping them together. He saw her undulations again and began an in and out motion. "It's time, darlin', up on your knees."

Henry took the plug and dipped it into the cream, making sure it was spread all over the full parts. He spread her apart again and pushed it against her. It entered her about half an inch. "All right, baby, it's going to feel too wide for a minute, but you'll be fine. You can make it slide in easier if you push out."

He continued to push, and when she started to make noises of complaint and discomfort, instead of taking it slow, he pushed it fully in.

"Oh!" she whimpered.

"There now, darlin', just be kind of still and get accustomed to it. Flex your muscles and feel it." He increased his pressure on her swollen bundle of nerves with one hand while the other went under her to tease a breast.

She started making louder noises, the ones Henry knew so well. He smiled to himself when her hands took the sheet into her fists and she repeatedly clenched and unclenched them.

"Spread a little more, darlin'. Make room for me."

When he entered her, she cried out loudly and began pushing back against him immediately. It wasn't long before her fists pounded the bed and she arched back, her head jerking back as she called out his name. Henry finished right when she did then collapsed on the bed beside her.

———

"HARRIET SAID SOMETIMES Arthur makes her sleep with the small plug. Do you want me to?"

"No, especially not your first time. I'll take it out in a few minutes and wash it off. Why does he make her sleep in it?"

"To remind her he's in control."

He considered that. "Hmm. Would you sleep in it if I wanted you to?"

She looked up at him and grinned. "Of course, I would. Besides, you told me once that in some situations, I need to call you *sir* and obey."

"I did say that, didn't I?"

"Yes, sir."

She settled down into the crook of his arm for a few minutes, drowsing until he roused her so he could remove the plug.

———

THE NEXT DAY, they just lazed and walked about the streets near the hotel. Henry wore his gun belt as he always did, and that day, Opal dropped her Derringer in her pocket, just to feel a little safer.

Henry laughed when they passed a hardware store that advertised a full line of plumbing products, saying it was apparently in the stars that she should have her hot running water.

They went inside and after conferring with a couple of the workers, determined the complete list of things they'd need to update their house. There was quite a list, not the least of which was a sizable boiler. He paid and arranged to pick up the items just before leaving for home. He didn't want them to be stolen from the wagon while it was at the livery.

"I don't think I'll ever be ready for this honeymoon to end," Opal said as they walked some more.

"It has to, darlin', or we'll never get hot running water at home."

"Don't need it if we stay here."

He laughed. "Yes, you got me there. I'm having the best time, too, all because of you. But I think I'll be ready to leave after a few more days."

"I imagine I will, too. But I want to wring every bit of fun out of our time here."

"You're doing a fine job so far. Lord knows you've wrung me out a few times."

"You've turned me into a trembling limp dishrag just as many times."

"I believe I'll do it again tonight."

"Good plan. Hey," Opal said, "don't we still have time to go to a matinee of that play we wanted to see?"

Henry pulled out his pocket watch and checked. "I believe we do. It's a few blocks farther out. Are you all right with that?"

"Yes, I am. I won't let those monsters keep me from enjoying my life."

He kissed her and gave her a quick hug. "That's my good girl."

On the way to the playhouse, Henry marveled at how this trip seemed to have worked wonders for her mindset.

THEY ENJOYED THE PLAY, a comedy, and decided they wanted to see it again before they left for home. It was getting late, and once outside, they began to discuss supper.

"I'm in the mood for a steak," Opal said. "Is that steakhouse Reed mentioned anywhere near here?"

"I believe it is, but it's still farther out. Is that all right?"

"I think so. I have my gun. You have yours. And it's turning out to be a nice night for a long walk back."

Henry agreed and put out his arm for her to take.

***

THEY WERE SEATED in front of one of several large planters that had tall plants growing in them. They created smaller, more intimate sections, rather than having one huge, open, loud eating area. The waiter brought out water glasses and coffee cups and a basket of various breads and butter. Henry and Opal looked at the menu and made their choices. She commented that the place was probably a cattle baron's dream as every possible cut of beef was offered.

They started in on the bread and made small talk. Opal said somebody ought to open a bakery in Big Rock because she'd enjoyed the ones in Rawlins. "It could be right next to Mary's restaurant. Oh, she could even serve their baked goods. Isn't that a good idea?"

He thought about it. "That's an excellent idea, Opal. Maybe you should open it yourself. You're a wonderful baker."

"Oh, hoot," she said as she waved her hand at him. "I've never made any of those fancy breads like we bought the other day. Why, I'd never even seen some of those pastries."

"All you need are the recipes, darlin'. You'd be a natural."

She didn't think so.

"You should think about it."

"I'd rather stay home and just be your wife."

"Well, I like that idea, too."

"Besides, how would you like it if I came home from work too tired to, um, wring you out?"

"Now that you mention it, I do like having you at home." He winked at her.

"I thought so."

The waiter brought out their steaks and potatoes and freshened their coffee.

Just as she was about to cut her steak, Henry saw the color drain from Opal's face. She grabbed his hand and darted her eyes, inclining her head slightly. He looked in that direction and saw what had her upset. Walking toward them was a group of men being led by a waiter to a table somewhere behind her. One man had a big red birthmark on the back of his right hand.

As they passed, Opal couldn't help but notice they looked like every other customer. They were neatly dressed, well-groomed, and anyone who saw them might assume they were business associates, or simply friends, out dining together.

Henry took her hand and called her name softly, "Opal, sweetie, look at me. Take a deep breath. I don't think anything's going to happen here at the restaurant. We'll be fine. Another deep breath, there, that's better. You'll be fine. There now." He smiled at her. "Better go ahead and cut into that ribeye. It looks way too good to let it go to waste."

She took another deep breath and nodded. She added a heap of butter to her baked potato and sprinkled just a bit of salt on it, then she slowly picked up the steak knife again and cut a piece of meat.

"Now taste that and tell me how good it is."

Opal smiled back at him. "It's perfect—nice and tender."

With a bite still in her mouth, she leaned over to get Henry's attention. "Should we alert somebody? The marshals? Or Deacon and Reed?"

"We don't know where they are. We can tell the Snows when we get back to the hotel."

"But these men'll be gone by then. They might lose them. Maybe we should follow them, or at least watch to see where they go."

"Opal, I'm not letting you get in harm's way. We'll be fine if we just eat our meal and leave quietly. You said you never really saw that man's face, and that means he didn't see you, either. They already passed by and didn't notice you. Now eat."

She frowned, but she ate. She couldn't carry on a conversation because she strained to hear anything they might say. She only heard murmurs and a few words or phrases here and there, but she heard enough to know that one of the men spoke with an English accent. Henry stopped trying to carry on a conversation with her.

It wasn't long before Opal and Henry saw two men with badges coming from the other direction, out of sight of the murderers. As they neared, they saw that Reed and Deacon were with the marshals. They all four sat at a table, still out of sight of Malachi Stone and his men.

Opal's heart beat fast and Henry got a concerned look on his face. He pulled one of his pistols out of his holster and placed it on the table beside his plate. When Opal saw that, she did the same with her Derringer.

They continued to eat, but warily. At one point, Deacon Snow's eye caught Henry's. Deacon briefly raised a finger to his mouth in a gesture that indicated to Henry that he should lay low and not show recognition. Henry gave a nod to no one in particular, to let Deacon know he got the message.

The waiter came around with a fresh pot of coffee. As he

topped off their cups, he casually reminded them to save room for fresh, hot apple pie.

"Oh, no, I couldn't possibly," Opal said politely.

The waiter moved on and Henry continued eating. Opal ate some, but mostly pushed her food around with her fork. Her stomach was tied in knots, wondering how soon she could put distance between the men and herself. As much as she wanted to follow the men and see where they were staying, she wanted even more to get back to the safety of their hotel room.

It wasn't long before the marshals and the Reeds rose from their table, and each one had a gun in his hand. Henry instinctively put his hand on the grip of his pistol. Opal saw him and picked up her gun.

The lawmen made their move, and they made it fast. Behind her, Opal heard one of the marshals yell, "Get your hands up! You're under arrest."

She heard a scuffle and heard one of the men yell, "Get him!"

A man came running up beside her, and she saw the birthmark. Without thinking, she lifted her arm and shot him in the knee, dropping him on the spot. He let out a yell of pain.

By then, Deacon arrived and secured the man's hands behind him. He tried to get the man to get up, but he couldn't with his injured knee. Henry stood and helped Deacon get the man on his feet.

The other three restrained men were brought to where the injured one stood. Deacon lifted his hand to stop their captors from letting them walk forward any farther.

"You should meet the one who brought you down," Deacon said, nodding toward Opal.

She stood, squared her shoulders, and went to stand before them.

"You shot me? A woman?" Jed asked, panting and grunting from his leg pain.

"My name is Opal. I was on the stage that day."

"You're the one!" Malachi blurted out. "We were coming after you next."

"You killed ten people, one of them a fourteen year old girl. What kind of men are you? I was nothing but the eleventh person to you. Because I struggled to survive and made it home, the law knew who to look for. You'll all hang for what you've done, and you deserve no less." She turned and went back to her seat at the table.

Henry smiled at her. "I'll help them outside, then I'll be right back."

A man from a nearby table walked up and offered to help Deacon with the lame man so Henry could sit back down with his wife. Henry took him up on it.

Applause broke out at nearby tables and spread across the room, everyone with their eyes on Opal. Some came over and asked to shake her hand and thank her.

When the uproar died down, their waiter, who had been standing by this whole time, came up to their table. With a big grin on his face, he asked if there was anything he could get for them. "Anything at all," he said.

Opal looked at Henry and her eyes twinkled. "Why, yes, you can. Please bring me a big ol' piece of that hot apple pie."

"Make that two," Henry said.

The waiter nodded and ran off to fetch them.

"I'm so proud of you, I can hardly keep from grabbing you and kissing you right now," Henry said.

"You'll have plenty of time to do that later."

"Count on it."

The pie was brought and while the waiter was still there, a

man from two tables over walked up. "Young man, please bring me their tab when they leave. I'd like to buy their meal."

As Henry was about to object, the waiter spoke up. "Oh, no need, sir. Their meals are already on the house." He looked at Henry. "Tonight, and every time they ever come back in here."

Opal chuckled and shook her head. She shrugged. "Thank you both."

THAT NIGHT as they lay in bed, Henry kissed her yet again. "How do you feel about all this now?" he asked.

"I feel so much relief, I'm almost giddy. I should probably feel guilty for shooting Jed, but I don't. It's possible they might have caught him before he got away, even if I hadn't shot him."

"You heard all that applause. Everyone there was glad you shot him. It was the right thing to do. You took away his chance to escape. If you hadn't shot him, Deacon probably would have, and his would have been a killing shot. This way, he has to face justice. You definitely did the right thing."

"Oh, I hadn't thought about that. I guess you're right. I feel like we can get on with our lives. I know I've come a long way, but until tonight, I've still had that nagging feeling that I'd never be safe until they were caught. Now I think I can finally put it behind me."

"We'll probably have to come back for their trial."

"I can do that."

"Will you want to watch them hang?"

"I don't know. I'll have to think about it. That must be an awful thing to witness."

"Sweetie, you've seen worse."

"I have; that's for sure. Still, I'll have to think about it."

"All right. I just can't tell you how happy I am that you're doing so well."

Opal turned and propped herself up on her elbows, looking intently at him.

"Do you think Deacon and Reed would be willing to drive our rig home?"

"Why would they need to do that?"

"Because I want to ride the stagecoach."

Henry grabbed her into a hug and rolled them over to the other side of the bed.

"This is wonderful, darlin'! I'm sure they'll do it."

Opal laughed. "I didn't realize it meant so much to you to ride the stage."

"Oh, hang that stagecoach. I couldn't care less about the stage. But, baby, this means you're letting the hurt go. You won't have this dark cloud over your head anymore. You're free of it now."

"I think I am. Now, maybe you can have the wife you originally expected, instead of the one you got. I'm a whole new woman."

"I think that means we need a whole new wedding night."

THE END

NORA NOLAN

Nora Nolan is one of my pen names. It's nice to meet you! I love to read all kinds of books. All kinds! So far, though, I've only written one basic type. They usually have fairly normal, sexy, fun relationships between the main characters, infused with a little wicked kink. So if you like age play, strong D/s lifestyles, or women in chains who beg to be caned, you might want to look for other authors. I'm not there yet.

My newest joy is sitting at the keyboard, letting the characters in my head write their stories. They often lead me in directions that surprise me. I never know when I start out what direction they'll take or where they'll end up.

I live in the southern central part of the US. My happier days find me with our family, or spending time with my wonderful alpha husband.

Email Nora directly at NoraNolan.books@gmail.com
Website: https://www.noranolanbooks.com

Don't miss these exciting titles by Nora Nolan and Blushing Books!

Operation Big Rock Brides (*Historical Western*)
Two Brides for Big Rock
Opal from Omaha

Big Rock Romance Series (*Historical Western*)

Marriage by Mail - Book One
A Badge in Big Rock - Book Two
Deputy's Dilemma - Book Three
Big Rock Rescue - Book Four
Bedlam at Big Rock - Book Five
Big Rock Romance Collection

BLUSHING BOOKS

Blushing Books is one of the oldest eBook publishers on the web. We've been running websites that publish spanking and BDSM related romance and erotica since 1999, and we have been selling eBooks since 2003. We hope you'll check out our hundreds of offerings at http://www.blushingbooks.com.

BLUSHING BOOKS NEWSLETTER

Please join the Blushing Books newsletter
to receive updates & special promotional offers.
You can also join by using your mobile phone:
Just text BLUSHING to 22828.